Hammond

A Western Novel by
Nolan Cordovano

1

You'll have to set aside emotion. And reason. These are the realms of man, and to judge us by these measures you might conclude that we have acted wrongly.

You are wrong.

This man came to us a killer. And a man like that, no matter that by a roundabout way his actions may have aided us, is nevertheless a sinner through and through, and whatever contract he has entered into with righteous men need not be honored.

There you have it. And if you do not believe that we are righteous, you are wrong again, for God blesses the righteous, and Lord Almighty are we about to be blessed. I can scarce put pen to paper when I think of what lies in that mine. And all of it for us. It near makes me giggle like a child.

But let me explain. It will only take a moment.

We left Bildsburg, Ohio in the year 1874. Sodom, I call it. The inhabitants are swine. They delight in the pleasures of the flesh. They take to drink, the women no better than the men, and when good and drunk they dance without inhibition; slovenly, the lust of animals pouring from their eyes. They swear. Filth pours from their mouths, accompanied by foolish notions; living free, obedient to nothing but the laws of man. And us they mocked.

I could lose myself detailing their wickedness, but I shall refrain. What you must know is that we left them to their devices. They can dance drunkenly through the gates of hell. As for us, we gathered up our earthly goods and set out west for a peaceful land all our own where we could live in proper adherence to the Good Book.

It was Reverend Mattick's idea. I supported it immediately. Some did not, and there you see how the wheat is separated from the chaff. But of those who did we numbered twenty-seven. We loaded our wagons and turned the mule's noses to the far horizon and not one of us looked back, for I tell you we feared to the depths of our souls that we might be turned to salt had we shown any yearning whatsoever to remain in that pit of iniquity.

We reached the New Mexico Territory in August of the year 1875. Nine of us. Why were we punished, you might ask. Why were those good souls lost? Good men and women. Children.

But consider this; that no more quickly had sorrow befallen us than the cave was discovered. Not a year had gone by. We had toiled, yes, to build our houses, to grow food in this barren land, and to find meat to feed ourselves. But we had survived. We built a church; this was most important. We even constructed a corral for the mules and horses, just along the creek bed God had led us to. Our five houses, the church, and the corral; it was enough to call a town. And then the Good Lord revealed to us a source of such riches so as to hurt your eyes.

It was Rose that discovered it. Rose Davidsdottir. I don't like Rose. I don't trust her. And neither should you. What she was doing traipsing around in the hills that day when she should have been at home cooking and caring for her hard-working husband I don't know. She was a dubious woman, I'll say that much. She possessed an earthly beauty, of which I am certain she was aware, and such beauty in the form of flesh and bone leads only to sin.

I never sensed a strong vocation from her, nor did she display equal enthusiasm for separating ourselves from the infidels back East. If any of us had turned for one last longing look at our point of departure it was Rose. Though I wouldn't know. I walked in front with Reverend Mattick.

But no matter who nor how, the discovery was made, and the spoils of the cave were meant for us all. Of that there was no question.

We nearly fell over one another that first day. I remember it well; all nine of us crowded into the dark narrow crevice cutting into the hillside. Simon Foster was the only one to have thought to bring a lantern and by its light we could see the vein as clearly as an April dandelion. It began on the rock face of the far wall, the gold intermingled with white quartz. A fissure had opened up beside it as wide as a man's fist and as tall as any of us. It ran farther than the light of the lantern would reach, and I swear to you there was more gold than rock in that seam.

We stuck our hands in it, so eager were we to begin. We scraped with our fingernails, unbelieving of what lay so close. Simon had brought with him a mallet from his house -- he's a smart man -- and by chipping away at the rock face alone, mined three ounces of gold in less than an hour's time.

We returned shortly with better tools. The quartz could be crushed easily enough, but the hard rock surrounding it would not break away with what we had, and after three days of near constant work, nearly all that lay waiting in the fissure remained out of reach.

The necessity of traveling to Santa Fe resulted inescapable. It was dynamite that was needed. Dynamite, pickaxes, materials to construct a sluice, and all manner of odds and ends, none of which we possessed.

Admittedly we had set out from Ohio to establish our own land of piety, and quite opposite was the notion of interacting with outsiders. But there was little argument. It was, after all, a gift from God, and chosen by Him were we to receive this mountain of wealth.

The Reverend volunteered to drive the wagon. I would have accompanied him, but I had come down with a cough and did not feel I had the strength to make the trip. Instead we chose Paul Conner. Perhaps that was our error. Paul is a braggart. It is his weakness. He is also impulsive. He acts without thinking, suddenly and impetuously. When asked about their purchases, he did not hesitate in bragging of the cave, which by this time we were already referring to as our mine.

But I should not blame him. I blame instead the greed of men. And how did we think we would escape it? Even had he kept his mouth shut, only one conclusion could be reached by the nature of the tools they bought. When two strangers arrive to town in a wagon in search of dynamite and pickaxes, ready to pay with freshly-mined gold, the devil is set loose.

They led them right back to us. How could they not? They had no way of eluding them. They led them back to our sanctuary, our land of refuge, like dogs on the scent of a bitch in heat.

And dogs they were. Eight of them, rough and filthy and bent on violence. Far worse men than ever we had laid eyes on in Bildsburg. They took the mine from us and nothing there was we could do to stop them. We are not a gun-toting lot. We are peaceful and God-fearing, and these animals descended on our small village to rob us without mercy.

You can imagine these men. They were unshaven. They stunk of unwashed bodies, and clothing unchanged and unwashed and covered in grime. They wore guns -- all of them. Some carried two; one on each hip. They spoke crassly, their voices rough and grating and poor in grammatical construction. Profanity laced their utterances more thickly than the gold running through the vein. It took us aback, though we pressed our case diplomatically. On those grounds we were correct. But these men did not live by the laws of justice, or what is fair and good. Certainly not by the laws of God. These men lived by violence.

They taught us this when they beat Paul down in front of us.

We had confronted them, the men of our group, outside the mine where they had set up camp. We had rehearsed what we planned to say to them, and quite firmly did we stand in our assertion that the mine was ours and these men had no business but to depart and leave us in peace.

Paul Conner delivered the message. He was a talker anyway, a gift often paired with boastfulness, and it took no prodding for him to volunteer for the task. He was eager to exercise his tongue, and I'm sure he was filled with confidence as we all were, knowing in our hearts we had been chosen to receive the gifts of the mine.

I told you already though, these men were unconcerned with justice. Before we had presented the totality of our petition they lashed out at him. They beat him with their fists, laughing as they did so, and when he lay limp and bloody in the dust we carried him back to town with their foul speech berating us all the while.

That is how it came to be that we gathered in our church two weeks later, all nine of us, to find a resolution to our predicament. Reverend Mattick oversaw the meeting. His wife Ruth had brought a pitcher of water, fresh drawn from the well. Vander Davidsdottir was there with Rose of course. Simon and Mary Foster were present, and myself, seated in the only pew yet built. Paul Conner and his wife Sara arrived late, I remember. Paul's wounds had healed and left no mark save for a bitterness for which I do not blame him.

After prayer we opened ourselves to discussion. Any ideas were welcomed. Any at all, urged the Reverend.

We sat in silence. No one had any.

Not any reasonable anyway. Mary Foster put it forth that we should return to the mine and demand that the men abandon camp.

'It's ours,' she insisted. 'They can't just take it from us.'

'They already have, Mary,' said Reverend Mattick.

'But if you just explain to them--'

'Did you not see my husband?' interjected Sara Conner. 'They almost killed him! And you want to send him up again?'

'I just thought--'

'They have guns!' Sara's voice had risen.

'Ladies,' said the Reverend. It was all he said, though I wished he would quote First Corinthians. This, I thought, is why women should stay silent in church. Reverend Mattick turned to me then.

'Amos,' he said. 'You've been silent. Do you have any ideas?'

I shifted in the pew. 'They do have guns,' I said, 'and they've shown they have no qualms about using violence. Paul still has his life, but if we go up again that might not be so.'

'We get guns then,' blurted Vander.

'And then what?' said Simon.

'Shoot 'em.'

'Who, you?'

'All of us.'

'I've never shot a gun before in my life.'

'I have.'

'You're going to shoot them Vander?'

Vander Davidsdottir grumbled something unintelligible. I have often suspected the man drinks. But that is inappropriate of me. He's a good Christian. He doesn't drink; he is simply dim-witted.

'I'm certainly not going to shoot anybody,' continued Simon. 'Are any of you?'

'Don't be foolish, Simon,' said Ruth Mattick. 'None of us are murderers.'

'I know that,' said Simon. 'Does Vander?'

'Stop it now, of course he does.'

'Somebody's got to shoot them,' piped up Vander again.

'Calm down everyone,' said the Reverend. 'Buying weapons is not the answer.'

'Then what is?' said Sara. 'An eye for an eye. Have you forgotten what they did to my husband? They nearly killed him. I think Mr. Davidsdottir is right. Somebody needs to shoot them. It's the only way.'

'Now Sara--' the Reverend started.

'What then?' Sara interrupted. 'What's your idea? Well, Reverend? What about you Amos? Simon?'

'What about the law?' Ruth Mattick asked.

'What about it, Ruth?' said the Reverend. He bristled at the suggestion of his own wife involving the law. Reverend Mattick had no respect for the law's of man. The Law of God. That was what he preached, and that was what bound us together. We had come west for it.

'I just thought...' his wife muttered. 'We need to do something.'

Simon Foster was shaking his head. 'It's useless. There is no law around here. There's barely any in Santa Fe. Even if we could get someone out here, we have no deed to that land. No one has filed a claim. None of us own it. And say we did. What kind of lawman is going to stand up against those men? There's eight of them. It's a sure way to get shot is all.'

We sat in silence again. The water pitcher sat untouched.

Neither Rose nor Paul had spoken. That was customary for Rose. She rarely talked to us. It made me uncomfortable. I think she thought she was better than us. Or different. Something. She was like an outsider in our group. Of weak vocation, I believe I've already stated. She looked at me suddenly and I turned my eyes away from her, for I had been staring at her bosom. I blushed, somewhat upset with her, for this is how a woman leads a man's mind to sin.

I looked at Paul. It was uncustomary for him to remain silent so long. He was the most talkative of us all, glib with his words and rarely self-censored. He stood against the church wall, watching us with a smile on his face. Almost like he was enjoying the discussion.

Maybe it was my attention on him, I don't know, but gradually the others noticed him as well, and soon we were all looking at him and that wry smirk on his face. It grew even wider as more eyes landed on him, and he began to chuckle giddily to himself.

'Ok Paul,' said the Reverend. 'You've got something to say. Say it.'

'I'm thirty steps ahead of you all,' he grinned.

'Go on.'

'Those men up there,' he pointed at the church window in the direction of the mine, 'are evil. Am I wrong?'

'No, you're not wrong.'

'And to evil men, evil happens. Don't it say that? The Good Book?'

'Yes.'

'And they stole from us.'

'Yes.'

'And they'll kill us if we try to take it back. They said that flat to our faces.'

'Yes. They did,' the Reverend nodded.

'They're wishing death on us.'

'Yes.'

'Well we'll put death on them.'

'How so, Paul?'

'I got word of a man.'

'You got word of a man?'

'That's right. In Santa Fe.'

'A man in Santa Fe?'

'No, he ain't there. He's up north a bit. But they told me about him in Santa Fe.'

'When was this?'

'Last week. I rode in.'

'You rode into Santa Fe?' the Reverend's question came out hard and startled Paul. It took the smile off his face. No one was supposed to go to town. This is what I meant about Paul. He is impetuous. Short on self-control.

'It wasn't just me,' he stammered. 'Vander came with me.'

All eyes turned on Vander. He stared back with his mouth open. Rose sat beside him saying nothing. No defense of him, and no support. Like she wasn't even there.

'Paul…so that's where you two were,' said the Reverend, but such was his consternation he had nothing with which to follow it.

'Well, we got to do something, don't we?' said Paul. 'I don't much like getting beat like that. None of you took a beating. How would you all like it?'

We looked away from him. It was true.

'So who is this lawman you're talking about?' said Simon.

'Well he ain't exactly a lawman,' said Paul. 'I mean, he is, but it's not always official. They say he's a man who can clean up a town.'

'What kind of a man does that?' asked Simon.

'I don't know. This one does.'

'You're talking about a hired gun.'

'No, a lawman. That hires his gun out.'

'I don't like it,' said the Reverend. 'Who told you about this man?'

'The Sheriff there.'

'The Sheriff in Santa Fe?'

'That's why I'm saying he ain't just a hired gun. He's a true lawman. The Sheriff vouches for him.'

'He's a killer.'

Paul didn't answer. He stood against the wall and dug his boot toe into the ground.

'You're suggesting we invite a killer into our town,' said the Reverend.

'Well, he'll do it. It's something.'

Silence came back to the room. I could not help but let my mind wander to the mine. Those men were taking that gold out as we spoke. Our gold.

'Vander,' I said. 'You were there. What impression did you get?'

Vander stared open-mouthed. He blinked slowly. Dim-wittedly. 'I don't know,' he said. 'He costs a lot.'

'How much?' I asked.

Vander looked over at Paul standing against the wall.

'Five hundred dollars, generally,' said Paul.

'Five hundred dollars?' repeated Ruth Mattick.

'That's generally. The Sheriff, he helped us get a telegraph off to him. He explained who is at the mine. I guess they call themselves the Jones's or the Jones gang or something. Anyhow, the man got back same day, quick like.'

'What did he say?' asked the Reverend.

Paul dug his toe into the dirt floor again. 'Said he wants five thousand dollars.'

There was a moment where we all stared at Paul Conner without speaking. The request seemed absurd, and at the same time not a one of us had any idea what the fair price of such an arrangement should be.

'That's preposterous,' said the Reverend finally. 'Where are we to come up with five thousand dollars?'

'There's that much in the mine. Easy,' said Paul.

'That's our money,' said Mary Foster.

'I agree,' I said. I hadn't planned on speaking, but the feeling was too strong within me. It felt wrong; this man whose name I did not even know, requesting such a sum of money. Our money.

'Even five hundred seems unsightly,' said the Reverend.

'I earned fifty dollars a month in Bildsburg,' said Simon Foster. 'And that's blacksmithing. Five hundred dollars is nearly a year's wages. Five thousand now...'

'It's unchristian what this man is charging,' said Mary.

'You're right Mary, it *is* unchristian,' said Ruth Mattick.

'Well that's what he's charging,' said Paul. 'Nothing we can do.'

'We can pay him what's fair, that's what we can do,' said Mary Foster.

'What's fair?' said Ruth.

'Well what would the Good Samaritan charge?' Mary directed her question at the Reverend.

The Reverend nodded. He had his hand to his chin with a finger curled over his lip the way he did when deep in thought. I respected the Reverend. He was a smart man. He would know what to do.

'The Good Samaritan,' he replied, 'did not charge for his help. That is the lesson of the story.'

'So this man shouldn't be charging anything at all,' said Sara Conner.

'No,' said the Reverend. 'This man clearly has been given a gift from the Lord. If it is his trade to clean up towns, as Paul says, and has had success at doing so, as seems to be the case, then he is a servant of the Lord.'

'It's almost like the Lord is bringing him to us,' Mary Foster said, her voice nearly a whisper.

'Indeed he is,' said Reverend Mattick.

Paul Conner tapped his boot toe nervously in the dirt floor. A divot was beginning to form where it landed. 'So what are we supposed to tell him?' he asked.

'Ride back into Santa Fe,' said the Reverend. 'Telegraph him. Tell him you'll give him whatever he asks for.'

'Five thousand dollars?'

'It doesn't matter. Once he has arrived and he sees our predicament, the Lord will touch his heart.'

'Reverend,' said Sara, 'we can't give him five thousand dollars. That gold is ours. You said so yourself, that is our gift from God.'

'Calm yourself, Sara. Understand this, all of you. The Lord works in mysterious ways. He has sent word to us of this man, a tool, if you will, chosen by God to unleash his fury on the men bent on robbing us. The Lord will not let this man take what is ours. As I just said, the Lord will touch his heart. You will see. No sooner will he arrive than he will forget all about the gold and his five thousand dollars, for he has a higher calling; to help God's chosen people reign victorious over the sins of the pagan.'

I exhaled. I had not realized I had been holding my breath, and when it came out a rush overcame me and I felt joyous. The same feeling came over all of us. I could see it in their faces. I nearly laughed, so relieved was I from the stress of it all.

'Reverend Mattick,' I said, standing from the pew and putting a hand on his shoulder, 'God has certainly blessed us with your wisdom.'

'Thank you, Amos. Paul, set out for Santa Fe in the morning. Simon, you'll go with him. What is the man's name?'

'Les Hammond.'

'Tell Mr. Hammond to arrive as soon as possible.'

2

Les Hammond turned the mug of coffee by the handle and turned it back again. When he looked up Carl was still waiting for an answer. He reached again for the coffee handle.

'Les? You're not seriously considering this are you?' Carl repeated the question.

'It's five thousand dollars, Carl. Hard to take your mind from it.'

Carl stood up and walked to the front door. He opened it and stuck his head out, then closed it behind him and sat back down on his cot.

'Prying ears in this town,' he said.

'No one's paying much attention,' said Les.

'You bet they are. They want us out. You can feel it.'

'That's how it always is. They beg you to come, but once you've done the job they can't get rid of you fast enough.'

'Why is that? You'd think they'd be building statues to us. Instead they're showing us the door.'

'These people want law and order, Carl. They want an end to violence. It's the same everywhere. Same with this town here. We gave them the law and the order, but now that the trash has been driven out we're a constant reminder of the violence that was. It's unsettling to them I guess.'

Carl shook his head. 'Well, like I said, I'm through with it. This was my last job. I'm too old for this.'

'Shit. You're thirty-one.'

'Thirty-two.'

'Young buck,' Les said, smiling behind the coffee mug.

'I'm getting old, Les. You too.'

'What else am I going to do?'

'Get yourself a woman. Settle down. What normal folks do.'

'That's why you're through. You ain't getting old. You got a taste for a woman's cooking.'

'Don't you put the blame on her. And maybe I have. She cooks real nice. I'd rather die an old man with a belly than shot dead in some no-name town, and that's where you're headed if you keep doing this. You make your living by the gun and you make your dying that way too.'

Les went back to playing with the coffee mug.

'You're getting me off track,' said Carl. 'Back to this nonsense. You said that telegraph came straight from the Sheriff in Santa Fe?'

'You mean the first one?'

'Yeah.'

'Came in right as I was walking past the telegraph office. Said there was some group of settlers out in the middle of nowhere went and got themselves tangled up with the Jones boys. A couple day's ride from Santa Fe.'

'And you responded right away. Told them you wanted five thousand dollars.'

'Yep.'

'Cause you knew nobody'd take you up on it.'

'Yep.'

'Because you want out of this business just as much as I do.'

Les rocked the mug back and forth on the small table in front of him. He breathed slowly.

'Les? Or are you going to tell me you like sleeping on a cot in a ten foot cabin listening to me snore all night? And getting shot at, no less.'

'Yes. I want out.'

'Ok. So then today. They get back to you.'

'Yep.'

'The Sheriff again?'

'The Sheriff. Says they'll pay the five thousand. They want me out there immediately.'

'Les, that don't make no sense. For five thousand dollars they could buy themselves an army. Who are these people?'

'I don't know any more than you at this point.'

Carl stood up and went to the door. He opened it again and leaned out. Les watched him from his cot. He had finished the coffee.

'You say this is the Jones gang?' Carl shut the door behind him.

'That's what the Sheriff said in the telegraph.'

'There's eight or ten of those boys. They're bad men, every last one of 'em.'

'That's why it'd be nice to have you with me.'

'No. No, Les, I already told you, I'm out. I'm done. I'm marrying Nora and I'm buying a piece of land and putting down seed and hanging up the badge. I'm done. And even if I did go running off with you, we're talking bad odds. Real bad. Those aren't gamblers with an extra ace you're running out, those are killers.'

'We've run out bad folks before. Hell, we just did, didn't we?'

Carl shook his head. 'This is different. Those boys are going to stick together. They're not going to get run off so easy. You ride out there and odds are you won't ride back.'

Les didn't answer. He stared at the empty coffee mug sitting on the small wooden table beside his cot.

'Tell me what you're going to do,' said Carl.

Les looked up at him.

'Jesus,' said Carl.

'It's five thousand dollars. I can't say no to that. Hell Carl, I want the same thing you do. I want a wife and a house, and children running around. I'd like to buy cattle and start ranching, and go to a barn dance time to time and drink a glass of whiskey. But how am I going to do that with what I've got? We charge five hundred bucks, we split it in half, then we spend it all traveling around and sleeping in hotels. And what have I got? Nothing. And here's my chance. And it's a good thing we do. We help people. We run out the rabble and make a town right again so people can walk down the street and not feel like their women are going to get raped and their children shot. So here's one more town. One more group of folks who need help, and whoever they are they have the money to do it. Well, goddamn it, I'm going to do it. I'm going to run the Jones's off or get shot doing it. But if I do, why I'll buy that ranch and start those cattle grazing, and maybe even find me a woman who cooks as good as Nora.'

'And drink a whiskey with me at a barn dance.'

'Yes. And drink a whiskey with you at a barn dance.'

Carl touched the door handle but did not open it. 'You're mind's made up.'

'Yep.'

'When do they want you there?'

'Yesterday, I suppose.'

'Alright,' Carl said, standing up. 'You might not be a hugging man, but damned if I'll let you run off and get killed without a proper goodbye. Come here.'

They hugged, and Carl patted him on the shoulder and squeezed his neck, and then Les was out the door and Carl sat back down on the narrow cot in the ten by ten cabin and listened to the sound of his friend's footsteps gradually fade away.

3

Rose stepped through the doorway of the cabin in a near run. The sun had set hours ago and little light was to be had from the moon. She took several bounds over the brown sand of the desert floor in bare feet and stopped. She listened. She strained her ears so hard it made her eyes squint. She heard nothing but the wind blowing over sand. She stood there anyway, waiting, listening, her bare feet absorbing the cold from the ground.

Nothing.

She wondered to herself what he would look like. If he was a young man, or an old man, or if he would really come at all.

She hoped he wouldn't. No, she hoped he would, only that she could get to him first. She imagined running to him in the blackness of the desert night. Him, tall and silent on his horse, listening to her. She would warn him. She would tell him everything; their plans, their lies, the whole sordid story of their group. He would take her in his arms and lift her up atop his great horse and take her away from there, away from the Reverend, from Amos, from her drunk husband.

She put her ears again against the night. She heard nothing.

She could simply start walking. Just walk into the desert, away from them, into another world. The thought put a rise of hope in her chest, followed immediately by the formation of tears in her eyes, for she knew it was a fantasy. She would die in the desert. Or worse, they would find her still alive.

Six long years she had been with them. Six years a prisoner. When her father had left for the war she had known even then that he would not return. Most of them did not. Her mother knew it. She aged the day he left, and before the year was out she was dead. No causes, no sickness or injury or reason, just dead. Of old age they said. Of a broken heart she said. She had no more than forty-three years.

Her mind went over it again, standing there on the cold sand of the desert, the wind cutting through her dress. She reviewed the memories, searching for an alternate story buried within them. There was none.

She had found herself suddenly alone and without food and without a clue, and only recently become a woman. And then Vander came along. Or the Reverend anyway. She had not married for love. It had never crossed her mind. Love was something she dreamed about; Vander was about reality. He was about food on the table, and a roof over her head. That's what she had thought, at least. It resulted that he was more about liquor, of drunken outbursts and the feel of his large hand squeezing her face and slapping her into silence. Food, it turned out, was hard to come by.

She had been transported from her home of two loving parents into a small world of rules and rituals. This new world lived within her old world, but set itself apart from it. It was small; its members hypnotized and untrustful, each with a watchful eye towards one another and eager to report their transgressions to the Reverend.

She had thought of running away. Obviously. But a girl alone and without money, without a horse or a trade or anything at all had few options. Had one option, really. And she knew how that would end; impregnated by a stranger and kicked out of the brothel, used and older and just as poor.

She had thought of killing Vander. Killing him, murdering him, these words did not upset her. She viewed them as liberating words. It would be easy to do. He was in a near constant state of drunkenness. Hiding it from the others was his sole strength. It would be easy to run a knife blade along his throat while he slept. Or simply suffocate him.

But no sooner could her mind begin to align the details of such a plan, than it would skip ahead to the aftermath. What would follow.

Amos was next in line.

He was even worse. She could put up with the abuse, verbal and physical, that Vander dealt out. But Amos was another man altogether. He caused chills to run down her spine. Thinking of him, catching him watching her, staring at her body as though he already had seen what lay underneath her clothing and lusting in the memory of it. It nearly made her thankful she had Vander as an excuse.

She had always held out some bit of hope, some fantasy of a change that though she could not foresee, could nonetheless desire in some version of reality. That ended when they decided to move west. Until then she could just nearly bear it. She had made friends, sort of, with a couple of the women. The children were nice; they were innocent. But leaving Ohio had torn the group in two. The wheat from the chaff, as Amos would constantly repeat week after week as they crossed the wilderness by wagon. Something biblical. She could not keep track of it all. Nearly everything they said was something biblical.

It was something biblical that gave them reason to ration the water to the males first, women second, and children last. They had reached the Indian Territories after Missouri, completely beaten and ragged. They were like skeletons dressed in dirty clothing, seated atop creaking wagons drawn by boney mules on the edge of death. Water had run out. The fields of grass had turned from green, to brown, to sand, and finally dust.

The Reverend did not want for water. Nor his wife. She snuck it when no one was looking. Her husband let her. Rose had caught her unawares, but said nothing. It would do no good.

The children cried for water until their throats dried and their cries were choked off. The Reverend and Ruth had no children. Neither did she and Vander. One more small piece of her life to be thankful for. Amos had no children, though she knew he wanted them, and were Vander to die he would force himself on her until she bore him a son. This she also knew.

Everyone else had brought children with them. They had tried to do the right thing. Most of them. They tried to ration it, the men giving to their wives and children. But there was not enough. They died along the trail, and when they did they were thrown to the ground and left to rot under the sun and be picked apart by wild dogs. They had explanations of course. Something biblical. But she knew it was only because they were too weak and lazy to dig graves and perform a proper burial.

It was clear who did not share water with their children.

Simon and Mary Foster's two children were the first to die. They were perhaps the two most enamoured by the Reverend's teaching. They left their children's dead bodies in a dry arroyo, face up to the sun. The Reverend said some words over them and promised the Fosters a seat beside God's throne, and then the mules dug back into their yokes and the traces snapped tight alongside the shafts, and they left them there dead and still, eyes staring into the blue sky.

The Conner's children were next to go. There were no tears shed that time either. Not any tears from Paul and Sara Conner anyway. Rose remembered that. She had cried, and so too had other members of their party, but those people were dead now; left alongside the trail in clothing well faded by the sun. Or more realistically, torn apart by animals and scattered to the wind.

And now they were here. Two day's ride to Santa Fe, and not a soul until then to know of them. And her without a horse. Perhaps she should have escaped in Bildsburg. Life in a brothel might have been a more bearable existence.

It was cold. She wrapped her arms around herself and walked back to the cabin. She lied down alongside

Vander on the mat spread over the dirt floor and put a finger to her ear to muffle the sounds of his snoring.

She thought again of him before she fell asleep. Of Hammond. Of what he would do when he arrived. How he would react when he discovered there was no money. She thought of this, and as her consciousness drifted into the *tinieblas*, returned again to the vision of running to him in the night and being swept into his arms atop his horse and taken far away from there.

4

He came to us during the hottest part of the day. The time when no one goes outside and you can feel the shimmer of the heat waves directly on your face.

He rode out of the horizon and right down the patch of earth between our houses that we liked to call Main Street. Though it wasn't a street at all.

We saw him from the church window, Reverend Mattick and I. His clothing was the same color as the hillside out of which he rode, and as he neared I will not forget how every piece of him, from the hat shading his eyes to the leather of his boots seemed worn smooth. As if he had stood in a desert windstorm for an eternity, the yellow granules whipping over each part of his being and into every crack and crevice of his makeup, wearing him smooth, sanding him into a polished, even-toned, sun-faded figure riding a beast just as weathered as he.

Even the gunbutt protruding from its holster glistened in the sunlight, smooth as though polished by the desert sand.

He stopped in front of us and Reverend Mattick removed his hat. I did likewise.

'You must be Les Hammond,' said the Reverend.

'That's my name,' the man replied.

'I'm Reverend Mattick. This is Amos Dowdry. Please, come in, come in,' he said, motioning for the man to enter the church.

He swung down from the saddle and I saw his eyes take in the area around our church in search of a post by which to tie his horse.

'You can let your horse loose in the corral by the creek,' said the Reverend.

'Let's talk first,' said Hammond. He dropped the reins of the horse and let them fall to the ground. Simply let him loose in the street, no worry of where the animal might go.

He walked into the church in front of the Reverend and myself. Somewhat abruptly I think. I felt he should have allowed Reverend Mattick to enter first. Out of respect.

But this man Hammond was rough. Rough in his manners, as though the sand had worn those away as well. He walked right into the church and took his hat off and sat down so casually on the pew it was as if he thought he were in a saloon. He wiped the sweat from his brow with his hand and that seemed disrespectful. His actions were those of a man completely unconcerned that he was in a house of God.

I'm not sure how well my face hid these sentiments. The Reverend did a much better job, though I knew he felt the same. We had formalized and rehearsed what we planned to say to him, beginning by explaining God's calling and our journey west from Ohio, but the man's brusqueness we were ill-prepared for. His questions started immediately.

'You fellas the ones sent the telegraph?'

Reverend Mattick and I responded in unison, though his response was in the affirmative, and mine in the negative. We glanced at each other, flustered, and before we could clear up the matter Hammond spoke again.

'It was either you boys or someone else. Seeing as how you were expecting me with my name already on your tongues I'm guessing you had something to do with it. Which is it?'

'We sent it,' said the Reverend, forcing a smile.

'Or you had Sheriff McLawdry send it for you,' said Hammond. 'Seems that'd be more accurate.'

'Yes, the Sheriff provided assistance to us.'

'Didn't say much more than you fellas got mixed up with the Jones gang.'

'Yes, that is our predicament.'

'Hell of a predicament.'

'Please, Mr. Hammond,' said the Reverend. 'You are in the house of the Lord.'

He swung his eyes about as though it had not occurred to him, though he was clearly seated in a pew and we had hung the cross of Jesus Christ over the doorway and another over the pulpit.

'This is our church, Mr. Hammond,' I said rather pointedly.

'Nicer churches up in Santa Fe,' he said. 'What are you folks doing out here in the middle of nowhere?'

'Allow us to explain,' I said.

'Please do,' he said, and reclined against the pew with his arms stretched out over the back edge.

The Reverend did the talking. He covered much of what we had rehearsed, though not as smoothly as he delivered his messages from the pulpit. I believe he was somewhat perturbed by this man Hammond. By his rough mannerisms and the way he had taken charge so quickly of the reunion. I know I was. I felt as though we were answering his questions as opposed to him answering ours. He made me uncomfortable. The Reverend too. And us in our own church.

But Reverend Mattick did an admirable job given the situation. He explained everything from our exodus from Bildsburg to the discovery of the mine and how the Jones's had taken up violence against poor Paul Connor.

Mr. Hammond nodded his head slowly when the Reverend had finished.

'You folks have been through a lot,' he said.

'Yes we have,' said the Reverend.

'I'm sorry to hear about your losses along the trail. My condolences.'

'Thank you.'

'So this is all of you? I counted five houses and this church. That and the corral yonder, and the privy.'

Back to his questions, I thought. He had not so much as made the sign of the cross. His simple condolences, and it was back to business. Such are the ways of the men of this world.

'It is,' said the Reverend. 'Nine of us. A small community, but an earnest one.'

'How far away is the mine?'

'No more than three, maybe four miles. It's through the bowl to the northwest, along the ridge,' the Reverend pointed out the window.

It was at that moment I heard the crack of what I believed to be thunder, and I thought hallelujah, He has sent rain to this barren ground. But the man Hammond stole that hope from me.

'Sounds like they're getting to work,' he said.

'What do you mean?' I asked.

'That's dynamite going off. You hear it?'

'It sounds like thunder.'

Hammond laughed. 'There's about as much thunder out this way as there is rain. You fellows have picked an almighty dry spot of earth to call home.' He looked at us as though we might appreciate his foul humor, and on seeing the seriousness of our nature expressed on our faces, he lost his smile.

'About that cave you're mining,' he said. 'You own the deed, correct? You've filed with the County Records Office for a mining claim on that section of land?'

Reverend Mattick looked at me. The question was not one we had expected. It was a question rooted in worldly concerns. We had found the mine ourselves; God had borne witness to that. What more right did we need?

'I take it you don't,' said Hammond.

'No, sir, we do not,' said the Reverend.

'Alright.'

'But you understand that it was we who discovered it.'

'Yes.'

'And that those men calling themselves the Jones's have used violence against us to steal it from us.'

'I understand that.'

'We are men of Christ, Mr. Hammond. We are not accustomed to dealing in claims and deeds, and such things. Bureaucratic matters if you will.'

'The law is though,' said Hammond.

'That is why we requested you, sir. As I understand it, it is your business to correct what is unjust. Using the law as a guidepost.'

'That's pretty much the lay of it. I see you're worried, Reverend. Don't be. You boys found that mine plain as day and the Jones's went and took it from you. Anybody can see that. Yes, there are claims and deeds and what have you, but I don't need to see it all. The Jones's aren't the mining type. If you were to get a US Marshal or a judge or some such involved, why yes, you'd be obliged to produce the paperwork, and if you didn't have it you'd be shit out of luck.'

He glanced around as he swore, his eyes falling on the cross. I thought he might have the decency to ask forgiveness for defiling our place of worship with such language, but he did not. You see the type of man he is.

'But that is why you sent for me,' he continued. 'So let's speak clearly. No need for misunderstandings. You're asking me to go up against eight or ten men, every last one of them a thief and a murderer, and none of them bothered by the fact. You see the odds. That's why my price is five thousand dollars, and that price is firm. It's my life I'm risking, and it's not one I'd take if there wasn't one hell of a reason for it.'

Again with the vulgarity.

'Of course,' said Reverend Mattick.

'As for that money,' Hammond leaned forward in the pew. 'You have the total sum collected?'

'Yes, of course.'

'That's a lot of money. You know that. You have it in safekeeping? The Jones's get wind of that much cash floating around and you'd all be dead by morning.'

'It's safe,' said the Reverend.

Now do not misunderstand the Reverend's words. He did not mislead the man, for not a word he spoke was false. We did have the money, and it was safe. It was in the mine where we had left it, and all that was needed was for us to extract it from the rock. Besides, the Reverend knew these words were not of substance. This man had been sent to us by God, to help us in our moment of trial. God would turn his heart. There, in that moment, it was filled with greed; all this talk of money. By the end we knew he would rejoice and give thanks that he had been blessed with the opportunity to come to the aid of good Christian men and women. For true wealth is not the legal tender of mankind, but service in the name of Christ Jesus.

'Good,' said Hammond. 'Keep it safe. No sense paying me now. I get myself killed and the Jones's would just take it off me. Besides, I won't take payment until the job is done.'

The Reverend smiled and gave me a look out of the corner of his eye. As if to say-- there is the hand of God going to work.

His relief came too soon however; for the man Hammond continued in the next breath.

'As a matter of custom though, I'll need a ten percent down payment. A man's word and his handshake go a long way, but in terms of money I've learned that nothing puts skin in the deal like an upfront payment. You boys get me the first five hundred and I'll get to work. Until then I'll avoid eating lead.'

'Surely,' said the Reverend. 'I understand completely. Please, make yourself at home. You are our guest. Let the church be your home while you are with us.'

'I'll make camp outside.'

'Oh. Very well. As you wish. You must be hungry.'

'Thirsty more than anything,' Hammond cut in.

'Very well. You may lead your horse to the corral and set him to pasture. In the meantime Amos and I will fetch you a pail of water and a bowl of stew.'

We stood then, the three of us, and exited the church back into the sweltering heat of the afternoon sun. The man's horse stood against the shaded wall of the church. Hammond gathered up its reins and we watched him walk through the dust and into the shimmering heat in the direction of the corral.

'I don't like him,' I said to the Reverend once Hammond was far from us. 'He's vulgar.'

'As are all men in the West, it seems.'

'At least in Ohio they had enough manners to sit upright in a pew.'

'Easy now, Amos. Much rests on this man.'

'What aversion does he have to staying in the church? Does he really prefer to sleep outside?'

'I suspect he does not feel comfortable there...a man like that.'

'What of the down payment? So concerned with money he is.'

'Trust in the Lord, Amos. The Lord will provide.'

And He did. The Reverend was right, as he most often is. Not a full day had passed before our prayers were answered.

5

William Jones wasn't happy. Big Will they called him. He could well have gone by the name Brutal Will, Killer Will, any kind of Will that causes a man to choose his words carefully when addressing him.

Right now he was Angry Will. Nothing had gone right for them since leaving Santa Fe. The mine was real, there was that. But three weeks of sweating in the desert sun had gotten them almost nowhere. They had ridden out without equipment. They had figured they would use what the missionaries had bought. Or whatever they were. They most likely weren't missionaries, but his men didn't know what else to call them. They gave his men the creeps; their hollow, sunken faces and long beards, all of them dressed in such colorless worn rags you would wonder just what type of hell had befallen them.

But the fools had not bought half of what they needed, and not until reaching the mine and commandeering the wagon did Big Will discover there was no dynamite. A trip back to town was what it took to realize the dynamite was on order. Another week lost.

And then when it finally arrived and they attempted to use it, the blasting caps were defective. The wicks would burn down alright, but nothing would ignite. They were useless.

He set the boys to work with the pickaxes. It was all the missionaries had bought. No drivers or mauls or mattocks or pry bars. Not even gold pans. Just shovels, pickaxes, and some of the materials needed to build a sluice box. Fools.

He put the men to work anyway. They needed to be kept busy or they'd stay drunk round the clock. They complained. Ceaselessly. Their complaints started with that they hadn't adequate tools, and when he sent for them in Santa Fe they complained the work was too hard without dynamite. Why couldn't they wait? Why couldn't they use blasting powder? Could they go in to Santa Fe to visit the whores?

They wanted to spend the money on booze and women as soon as they dug it from the cave. He suggested they take the missionary women, but from what they had seen of the men, the idea gave them shivers.

The damn missionaries. Another problem. He thought long and hard of sending the boys down to kill them all. But word was already out that the Jones's were in the area. He didn't need random murders added to his wanted poster. He had given his boys one simple message:

none of the missionaries were to leave. No one in, no one out. But it had happened twice now, in the plain light of day. Someone running off to Santa Fe. Two of them each time. Causing problems, of that he was sure. He still had no solution for them.

And someone was thieving. He was certain of it. Almost certain anyway. They were pulling out gold, and it was real. And it was only the smaller flakes near the front. The vein ran back as far as light could be cast, along the edge of the fissure, gobs of it, waiting there so close. He stored what flakes they accumulated in a glass jar and slept with it cradled in his arms. At the end of each day he would parse out a divvy to the men. Evenly.

But there should have been more. He suspected they might all be stealing, pocketing nuggets here and there. That was the trouble working with thieves; they were thieves.

And now this.

Junior stood in front of him, his bottom lip hanging open. That lip always bothered Big Will, and it bothered him now.

'When did he ride in?' he said.

'Not but a few hours ago,' said Junior.

'And you're sure he's alone?'

'I'm sure.'

'Where is he now?'

'He's down there with them missionaries.'

'What's he doing?'

'I don't know, boss.'

Big Will dragged a finger along the side of his nose and into the stubble of beard. It was hot. The sun had begun its descent but it would be hours before the heat left.

'You see why I didn't want those goddamn missionaries riding back into Santa Fe? You see what's going on?'

'What's going on, boss?'

'They sent for help, you idiot. Frank, Donnie,' he shouted over his shoulder at two men loafing in the shade. 'Get over here.'

They pulled themselves up from the ground and waddled over to Big Will and Junior. Like two lazy dogs in the afternoon sun.

'Junior here says a man rode in this afternoon. Found his tracks.'

'Who was it?' said Frank.

'He doesn't know. Point is, we don't want anyone riding in or out. That means trouble.'

'What do you want us to do?'

'Ride over. Go see who it is.'

'You want us to shoot him?'

'See who it is first. If it's another one of those odd folks dressed up all funny with beards, leave him be. If it's anyone else, shoot him. Point is, no one's leaving.'

'Right now, boss?' said Junior.

'Yes right now. What the hell would you be waiting for?'

'It's hot.'

'I know it's hot, goddamn it. It's always hot. What the hell do you expect? We're in the desert you dumb son of a bitch. Now move it. You wait any longer and the sun will go down and you won't be able to see who it is. Get on now.'

Junior nodded, sending his bottom lip flapping over his gums, and Frank and Donnie mumbled to themselves in vain, for Big Will was done talking. He had turned his back on them and marched in direction of the gold cave.

The horses were no less reluctant to leave the shade of the hillside than the men. Nevertheless, horses and riders all trudged out into the desert sand with the sun to their backs. Their horses' hooves plodded away from camp and into a six mile wide bowl baked brown by the sun.

Out of sight from the cave, Frank pulled a small silver flask from his pocket. He took a long swallow and handed it to Donnie. Junior turned his neck towards them.

'What are you looking at, boy?' said Frank.

'Nothing,' said Junior.

'Yes you are. You're looking at us like you was one of those dumb missionaries making faces at a spit of liquor.'

'Big Will doesn't want us drinking.'

'Big Will,' Frank took another swallow. 'Kiss my ass,' he said, then glanced at Junior. 'You gonna tell him I said that?'

'No.'

'No is right.'

They rode another hundred yards, Frank and Donnie passing the bottle between them and laughing at something known only to them. Junior glanced back at them, squinting into the setting sun.

Frank stretched the flask out.

'Take a drink, boy. Go on. This is primo quality Santa Fe whiskey.' He jostled the flask.

'No,' said Junior.

'Don't want to upset Uncle Will? That it?'

'No.'

'Come on boy, share a drink with me and Frank. Less you don't cotton to us.'

'I'd prefer to stay sober.'

'Why's that, Junior?'

'Cause this is serious. And I don't figure on getting shot.'

'What the hell you talking about boy?'

'I'm talking about that man down there.'

'Hell, he ain't nothing to be afraid of. He's just one of them missionaries is all.'

'We don't know that.'

'We don't know that and we don't not know that,' Frank took another slam off the flask.

'Big Will's worried.'

'Big Will's got his knickers bunched up tight. Been acting scared as a laying hen lately,' he put the flask to his lips then ripped it away and frowned at Junior. 'You gonna tell him I said that?'

'No,' said Junior.

'No is right,' said Frank. 'Now close that lip.'

They rode in silence. When they had emptied the flask Frank shoved it back in his pocket. He said something to Donnie and Donnie gave a weak laugh.

A mile out from the five houses and church they pulled up and sat on their saddles looking over the desert with their hands at their brows, though the sun was low in the sky behind them. They sat for some time, watching nothing, then Frank turned his horse east.

They began a long slow arc around the town. They had completed a quarter of it when Frank pulled on the reins of his horse. The corral had come into view.

'You see that?' said Frank.

'See what?' said Junior.

'Down by the corral. Is that someone down by them junipers? Donnie? You see that?'

'I don't see too good,' said Donnie.

'I see him,' said Junior. 'I see his horse too.'

'Alright,' said Frank, nodding. 'Alright, we found him.'

He jerked his horse's neck around and drove his heels into its ribs sending it loping back the way it had come. The others followed a few yards until they were back out of sight from the corral.

'He doesn't look like one of them missionaries,' said Junior, once they had come to a stop again.

'You don't know that,' said Frank.

'They don't ride horses like that. Their animals ain't nothing but skin and bone.'

'Maybe,' Frank muttered.

They sat in silence and stared at the adobe houses far across the sand until Donnie spoke.

'Any whiskey left?'

'We drunk it,' said Frank.

Donnie snorted.

'What should we do?' Junior directed his question at the both of them.

'Drink,' said Donnie.

'Shouldn'ta drunk it so fast,' said Frank.

'You shoulda brought more.'

'Bring your own next time.'

Donnie snorted again and bent over and reached into his horse's saddlebag. He rummaged around and a clink sounded and he pulled out a clear bottle with what looked like piss in it. The cork pulled with a pop and he put his lips to it and tilted it back so air bubbles shot up through the liquid as it gurgled down his throat.

'You son of a bitch,' said Frank. 'You was just gonna drink all mine, wasn't you? Pass that over here.'

Donnie laughed, sloppily, and handed the bottle to Frank.

'What about that man?' said Junior.

Frank paused with the bottle at his lips. He pulled it away a touch. 'What about him, Junior?'

'Well...that's what we was sent here for, wasn't we?'

'Yeah?' said Frank.

'Ain't we supposed to kill him?'

Frank looked at Donnie and back at Junior. He laughed. 'So go kill him, Junior. Best tuck that lip in though or he might go and shoot it off.'

They laughed, Frank and Donnie, so hard whiskey dribbled out of Frank's mouth and down his chin.

'Come on, Donnie,' Frank wiped his mouth with his sleeve. 'Let's sit by them rocks over there. You too, Junior. Come on.'

The two men drank with their backs resting against upthrust shards of rock and watched the sun set over the hills. Junior declined. He sat fidgeting with his revolver, checking the rounds and looking down the sight. He'd put it back in its holster and pull it out again, slowly, as if time itself was grinding to a stop. He drew the hammer back and released it and repeated the motions again.

'Alright, Junior,' said Frank. 'Night's coming on. Why don't you go shoot that bum before you go shooting one of us by accident.'

'Ya'll are coming too, aren't you?'

'Course we're coming. Get up, Donnie,' he stood up and kicked Donnie's boot. 'Goddamn drunk is falling asleep on us.'

They mounted up and rode in a half circle towards the corral, staying well shy of the houses. They rode in silence, save for the creaking of the saddles and the horses' hooves softly striking the ground, until Junior spoke.

'How are we gonna do it?' his voice carried in the dark.

'Do what?' said Frank.

'I mean, what are we gonna say when we get there?'

'We ain't gonna say nothing. Just walk up on him and shoot him.'

'Just like that?'

'Just like that.'

Junior nodded, though no one could see him in the dark.

A deep red glow of dying coals could be seen a hundred yards out. The men pulled their guns out. They did not slow their pace or spread out, they simply rode up to the corral fence, which consisted of nothing more than chicken wire staked into the ground, and dismounted. Donnie put a foot to the chicken wire and it caved inwards. It bent easily, taking one of the stakes with it. Approaching the coals they could make out a bedroll laid out along the ground.

'You there,' said Frank, his voice loud in the still air. 'Get up.'

As they neared the coals they saw the bedroll was empty.

'Ain't nobody there,' said Donnie.

'Anyone around?' called Frank.

'There is,' a voice came out from the junipers.

'Who's that?' said Frank, turning towards the voice with the gun pointed out from his hip.

'The man whose camp you just walked up on.'

'You one of them fellas with the long beards?'

'No.'

'Whyn't you come out where we can see you?'

'Holster your guns first.'

'We're just being cautious,' said Frank.

'So am I.'

Frank looked at Donnie, whose attention was consumed by the blackness in front of him. Junior stood behind them, gun drawn and breathing heavy.

'You gonna tell us your name, mister?' said Frank.

'I'm Les Hammond. I take it you're some of the Jones boys.'

'How'd you know?'

'You're the reason I'm here.'

There was a moment when all was still and quiet in the corral. Not even the wind blew. And then Donnie broke it. He was drunk, impatient, and when he heard the name he realized in that instant the true weight of the moment.

Fire stabbed out of his gun. He shot into the dark at Hammond's voice, and no sooner was the gun barking in his palm than his chest was pounded by bullets and he toppled backwards with his legs crumpled beneath him.

Frank didn't wait. He saw where the gunfire originated from and squeezed the trigger of his revolver, but only once, for Hammond's gun answered, sending a .44 caliber bullet into the soft flesh between his clavicles. It blew through the delicate anatomy of his throat and shattered the vertebrae in back of his neck as it exited. He was dead before his eyes had time to close.

Junior was running. His body collided into the chicken wire and he fell to the ground with it, cutting his face and hands and lunging back to his feet, his gun lost and his bottom lip hanging low on his panicked face. He found his horse and jumped to its back. His boots hammered into the animal's ribs, finding the stirrups afterwards, and he raced away from the corral with his body low against the horse's neck, fearing all the while the hard smack of a bullet in his back.

6

The sound of murder woke us. What else shall I call it? Not a full twelve hours since he had ridden into our sanctuary than he had defiled it by desecrating the seventh Commandment.

We came running; Reverend Mattick, Simon, Vander, Paul, and myself. The women were made to stay in the houses.

Ill-prepared we were to witness the horror the Devil had unleashed in our corral. Exactly what Mr. Hammond said I do not recall. Too taken aback was I to put attention on his words. What I do remember is his coolness. How calm he remained, as if taking the lives of two men were something routine.

By no means were we able to return to our beds that night. Not for sleep anyway. Except for Mr. Hammond. Lock your doors, was all he said. Lock your doors. As if we had locks.

I certainly did not sleep. I lay awake fearing our future; the only detail of certitude being violence. Before the sun had risen I left my house and walked. I prayed.

Soon the men came from their lodgings and we convened in the church. We were shaken, all of us, but the Reverend was our rock. He gave us direction. Bury the bodies he said; that was our first step. After that we would know what to do.

Hammond did not help. He remained in the corral, cleaning the rifle he had disassembled.

We carried the two men's bodies to the edge of town and dug their graves by our own labor. We took their belongings from their horses and went through them, for we knew not what names to write on their graves and we hoped some clue might be offered from them.

We did not find any. Soiled clothing and ammunition in the first, and then, to our surprise, a small pouch of gold containing surely at least an ounce. The going rate, as we understood it from those in Santa Fe, ran nearly thirty dollars to the ounce. More money that any of us had seen in a very long time.

The second satchel stunk worse than the first. We pulled out clothing that had forgone a washing for how long I cannot say. Beneath it was a bottle containing alcohol, which Vander took to the creek to empty.

And then the answer to our prayers. A glass jar so filled with gold it must have weighed at least pound. It was still rough, intermingled with quartz and rock, but there was no doubt as to the prize it held within. We held it up to the early morning sunlight and the joy of the Lord shone from our eyes.

Reverend Mattick held it before us and had us lay our own hands upon it.

'The Lord provides,' he said. 'He hath provided us with this man to take our enemies from us, and he hath provided this golden mineral to assuage the man's greed. A deposit he wants. A deposit we will show him.'

Vander returned from the creekbed and when we showed it to him he grabbed it and laughed, recklessly I dare say, drunk surely on the joy of God's deliverance.

We returned to the church and gathered there with the women and so merry were we with what we had found that we showed it to them and and found beauty in the grace of their smiles. Except for Rose. Her jubilation was found wanting. She stared at the jar with a solemn face, unable to share in our triumph. How I would like a moment alone with her. To chastise her. I must speak with the Reverend. If Vander cannot make a cheerful and obedient woman out of her, other arrangements should be considered.

Reverend Mattick passed the jar around, allowing each of us to hold it in our hands.

'How much is there, Reverend?' asked Sara Conner.

'A pound, surely. Perhaps more. Would you agree, Simon?'

Simon Foster nodded his head.

'Where will we keep it?' said Mary Foster. 'Should we bury it?'

'We must show it to Mr. Hammond first,' said the Reverend.

'But what if he takes it from us?' said Mary. The worry showed in her face.

'We will only show him,' said the Reverend. 'He has asked to see a sum equal to a ten percent deposit, and lo, the Lord has given us the means to do so.'

'But what if he wants to take it for himself?' Mary's distress continued.

'God will change his heart. He has already started the process, for Mr. Hammond has only requested to lay eyes upon the deposit. He will not accept payment until his job is done.'

'His payment is a place in heaven,' said Sara Conner, quite brusquely.

'Yes, Sara,' said the Reverend.

'And that's it.'

'Of course,' nodded the Reverend.

Paul Conner seemed nearly as anxious as his woman. He had started to pace back and forth, and interjected suddenly. 'What if he wants payment now?

For the two he shot? What if you show him the jar and he aims to keep it? What then?'

I had not considered this possibility, and from the faces of the others I suspect neither had they. We looked to Reverend Mattick, but he had no answer. It was then I found my voice, inspired by the Holy Spirit.

'The gold is ours,' I said. 'It is a gift from God. And so is this man who has come to rid us of the Jones's. He is a gift, but he comes in the form of a wolf in sheep's clothing. You see how quick he is to kill. You see the violence within him. In the end he is an instrument, a tool used by God to complete a task. That is God's decision. Just as it was God's decision to bless us with the wealth of this gold, it is His decision to choose this man Hammond to wield His power. God will bless him for coming to the aide of His flock. What reward lay in store for him we cannot say, for the Lord works in mysterious ways. But I tell you this; what sits in this jar, and all that lies in the cave is ours and ours alone. That is our reward for following the path of righteousness. Mr. Hammond will not take it from us.'

'Amen,' said Mary Foster.

'Amen,' said Ruth.

'That is the Lord's message that Amos has just delivered to us,' said the Reverend. 'God bless you, Amos.'

'Thank you, Reverend,' I said. I felt a smile cross my face knowing the good men and women's perturbation was eased by my words. A sense of satisfaction rested within me. But before I could bask in the warmth of that good feeling it was cut short.

A knock sounded on the church door and it swung open.

Les Hammond walked in, his revolver tied low in its holster on his hip, and a rifle in his hands. He had that same sand-polished look as the day before, perhaps more so. The colors of his clothing and his skin blended into one another to create a mix of tan and brown, their dullness accentuated by the glistening whites of his eyes around the pupils.

Those piercing eyes fell immediately on the jar of gold.

'Morning,' he said, and looked upon each of us individually, counting us. 'Everybody's here. That's good. And quick to round up the deposit too. Let's have a look.'

He held his hand outstretched to it, leaving us no option but to give it to him. He turned it in his hands and held it up to the light coming through the window.

'That should do it,' he said. 'Close anyway. All the rest of it look like this?'

'Yes, Mr. Hammond,' said the Reverend.

'You're keeping it in a safe place?'

'Certainly.'

'Good. Don't tell me where. It's best I don't know, just in case things take a wrong turn with the Jones's. Just as long as I know you've got it.'

'Worry not, Mr. Hammond,' said the Reverend.

The man set the jar on the pew and turned to us.

'Listen sharp now,' he said. 'They know who I am and they know why I'm here. They'll know it was you who sent for me, and that puts you all in danger. From here out things'll happen fast. I'll ride to the cave you've been mining. My aim is to get to them before they get to you. In the meantime I want you to gather up your guns and get back inside this church. Throw that drawbar in place. The adobe's thick on these walls and the windows give you a good line of sight. You can make a decent stand here if need be.'

'Are you suggesting we take up arms against these men, Mr. Hammond?' said the Reverend.

'Unless you prefer getting shot,' he responded.

'You misunderstand us then. We have no weapons. Even if we did we would not put them to such use; not for the killing of our fellow man.'

Les Hammond looked around at us. 'What do you figure on doing if those men come to town?'

'Our prayers will guide us,' said Reverend Mattick.

'You can pray all you want,' he said. 'But if the Jones's come for you I suggest you save your prayin' for later and send some lead their way. Those two dead boys you just buried left you a couple revolvers and a rifle. Now go and get some water from the well. Set yourselves up with some grub. Wish me luck.'

He turned his back to us and left through the church door. We were left alone. Nine of us and our jar of gold.

7

Big Will had to remind himself to relax his jaw. If he kept it clenched so tightly he would grind his teeth away. The dentist in Abilene had warned him of that. Relax, he had been told. The dentist didn't know what kind of fools he had to work with.

He had been so upset by the news he had nearly shot Junior. If it wasn't his own nephew he just might have. Dumb son of a bitch running off like that, letting Frank and Donnie take the bullets.

He hadn't slept much. After Junior had ridden up scared as a jackrabbit and given him the news with his big lip flapping, his mind began churning and wouldn't let up. Les Hammond wasn't just any man. There was a reason people paid five hundred dollars for him to restore law and order to their towns; he got the job done. He was fast with a gun, he put his bullets where he wanted them, and stayed cool when others lost their heads.

He had thought his luck was beginning to turn. The dynamite had finally come in. Good powder, working blasting caps, and long wicks. In just one day they had dug out more gold than they had in the previous three weeks. And now this.

Big Will stretched his jaw out and told himself to relax. Think it through. The decision was between riding to the missionary settlement or remaining by the cave and waiting. He wished the entire gang was together. With Frank and Donnie gone he was down to just six men, all of who were full of hare-brained ideas, none of them worth shit.

An hour after sunrise he had made his decision. He called for his men to gather round.

'Bill, Jody, you and me are riding down. You two,' he pointed to the Cupper brothers, 'stay here with the yellow-belly. Just pray he don't go running off if Hammond comes in shooting.'

The Cuppers began to protest, petitioning for Jody to remain with them instead, but Big Will cut them off.

'Shut up, both of you. Odds are he'll be in town. If he does come up this way he won't ride through the bowl; it's too open. Knowing Hammond, he'll ride west and turn north into the hills if he heads this way at all. We'll ride down that route and if he's left town we'll catch him.'

They mounted up with water in their canteens and enough ammunition to finish a small war. The Cupper brothers and Junior stood in the sun watching them go. When they had disappeared into the hills the brothers sat in the mouth of the cave where the shade fell and shoved tobacco into their cheeks. They did not offer any to Junior and though he enjoyed a plug of tobacco in his cheek from time to time, he did not ask.

Instead he pulled his rifle from the scabbard laying alongside his bedroll and walked eastward toward the bowl. The Cuppers did not so much as ask him his intentions. They spat tobacco from the cave interior and crumbled odd bits of quartz in search of gold flakes.

Junior felt the sun hit him as soon as he left the shade. It burned through his shirt and roasted his face where the hat brim's shade did not reach. He curled his bottom lip inside his mouth and bit down. It'd burn if he wasn't careful. One more thing for them to make fun of. He was tired of being the butt of the jokes. Tired of being called yellow. The feeling nagged at him that if he wasn't Big Will's nephew he wouldn't be part of the gang at all, and that everybody knew it.

He could change that with one shot. Ambushing a man from a hundred yards out didn't get the same respect as shooting one down with a revolver at close range, but considering their circumstances, he figured it'd take him pretty far.

Big Will was right; the bowl was open. Open enough that if Hammond rode through it, Junior would know. It also had just enough cover to give a man on foot a bit of concealment. Creosote grew in clumps, and patches of shadscale dotted the edge of the bowl.

He looked around. He needed something firmer, something on which to steady the rifle. He couldn't afford to miss.

He found it a quarter mile from the cave; a rock slab three feet high by two long. Next to it was a short stand of dalea. It's flowers were not in bloom, easing the worry that it might attract the eyes of Hammond. The rock slab was good. It was perfect. He lied down on his belly and nearly screamed when he felt the heat burn through his shirt. He fought through it until it dissipated.

He placed the barrel of the rifle over the rock and looked down the sight. His lines were excellent. He took it back down and stared out at the open desert bowl. The sun scorched his back. He edged closer to the dalea, but received no shade from it. Sweat dripped over his brow and he wiped it away with his fingers. The rock in front of him reminded him of the night before, when he had sat with Frank and Donnie in the stand of rocks and watched them drink as night fell. And now they were dead.

To hell with them, he thought, and wiped his brow again.

8

Les Hammond rode fast, his Winchester out. There was little fear of being dry-gulched, for the bowl of desert through which he rode was flat and featureless for nearly two miles. Not so featureless that he should let his mind wander, but there was no stopping it.

Those people. They gave him a chill, though the air was already hot from the rising sun.

The West attracted all types of people. The adventurous, the brave, entrepreneurs and outlaws. It also drew to it men and women such as these; crawled out from the darkest cracks of civilization, strange and removed and utterly incomprehensible. He could not shake their faces from his mind. The skin wrapped thin and tight around hollow eyes, stretching along the features of their skulls. Scraggly beards drooping from the men's faces, and all nine of them dressed in rags hanging from their scrawny bodies.

They had gone too long with too little food. Aged beyond their years.

There was the one though. She was too thin, as were the rest of them, but young, and pretty. He remembered how she had stared at him there in the church. Saying nothing, just looking hard into his eyes. He remembered how she had shaken her head at him. As if to say no, don't go. Or maybe it was his imagination.

Through the images of memory blending before his eyes he caught the glint of sunlight on metal. His body moved before his awareness had time to process it. A lifetime in the desert had ingrained the sights and sounds and smells of the landscape into his subconscious. Nothing reflected light. Not in the desert.

He jerked the reins to the right and leaned over hard. The bullet caught him on the edge of his left arm where the tricep meets the shoulder. It dumped him out of the saddle and as he fell he heard the crack of the shot catch up. His horse danced for a few yards and stopped and stood.

Hammond did not remain where he had fallen. He kept hold of the rifle in his right hand, rolled to his belly, and crawled to a clump of creosote. He did not stop when he reached it. He continued to crawl along the length of it. As he did so another shot clapped and echoed across the desert bowl. The bullet clipped the creosote. It sent flakes of dry leaves spinning and fluttering into the air.

Les Hammond stopped crawling at the edge of the foliage. He put his chin on the ground and peered up from under the thin branches. He had a better idea of the shooter's location than the shooter did of his. Both shots had come from a boulder sitting alongside a half-dead dalea bush. There was no way to leave that position without crossing flat empty space.

He eased the Winchester into the creosote branches and tucked the barrel into a crook of bark. He looked along its length and put the bead on the top of the rock behind which the shooter sat. He relaxed and let the waiting begin.

The desert returned to silence. The sun threw its heat on his back. His arm burned but he did not look at it. A lizard sprinted along the ground ahead of him but he did not move his eyes off the rock. The desert passed through time at a deliberative pace. Time crept imperceptibly along. It languished.

Hammond was accustomed to it. Few men were. He wondered if the shooter behind the rock was a consort of the desert, or an interloper setting foot momentarily within its domain.

Time would tell. And it did. The shooter's head peeked up over the rock slab, hatless, his eyes squinting into an expanse of brown and red dust. Hammond put the bead of his sight just below the man's nose. He

71

waited. A moment passed and the shooter pulled his rifle over the top of the rock. He edged up higher and swung his left arm around to steady the barrel. Hammond followed the man with his gunsight, waiting for the shooter to hold still.

His breath came in, it released, and as his chest fell to its apex of respiration he pulled the trigger and sent a .44-40 caliber bullet out of his rifle at nearly two thousand feet per second. It hit its target and the man's head disappeared behind the rock.

Hammond did not wait, instead rising to a low crouch, running with the sound of sand crunching below his boots and dropping behind a divot in the ground where hard rock jutted out of the desert floor. He reloaded and waited once more, time immeasurable, then crawled to the dalea bush beside the rock slab. The body lay behind it, the upper part of its head gone. Hammond slid the Colt revolver out of the man's holster and tucked it against his back through his belt.

The cave had to be close. He looked back at his horse standing alone. It was watching him. He let it be.

The ground rose in front of him in a slight grade up the hillside. He followed the shooter's tracks with his eyes. Their direction was clear. He rose again, this time bent only slightly, and sprinted thirty yards up the hill to a cluster of overgrown pincushion cactuses. A moment to catch his breath and he darted out again, holding the rifle in one hand along his hip. The slight elevation he gained as he ran allowed his sight to rise over the sloping ridge behind which were tied three horses, and a wagon with a canvas tarp tied from its sideboards and slanting down to where it was staked to the ground.

The boom of a gunshot cracked out from the hillside. The bullet whistled through the air past Hammond's head.

He swung the butt of the rifle to his shoulder and grabbed the forestock with his left hand. They had revealed their position; an opening six feet wide in the base of the hillside not far from the camp. He fired into it without coming to a stop. Still walking, he levered another round into the chamber and sent the spent casing toppling to the dust. He fired again, still moving, three steps, the repeating lever cranked and another round brought into place. He fired again. Three more steps, fire, three steps, fire.

He advanced with constant gunfire, not pausing until arriving within thirty yards of the camp, then running, crossing the distance in seconds. He turned upon reaching the wagon and sent two more shots into the cave mouth, then ducked under the slanted tarp. Not seeing what he was after, he turned to the wagon bed and scanned its contents. Sticks of dynamite sat in a wooden chest, wrapped in neatly stacked bundles.

He pulled a bundle apart and grabbed two sticks. The book of lighting matches sat next to the chest. He struck one and put the flame to the wicks. He held them in his left hand and raised the Winchester again to his shoulder, the left hand tasked with supporting the rifle barrel while simultaneously carrying two burning sticks of dynamite, pain shooting down his arm from the bullet wound along his tricep.

His shots were far from accurate, but they did have a six foot wide target. He continued to fire, counting down the rounds out of the magazine. Forty feet from the mouth of the cave he let go of the rifle barrel with his left hand and flung one of the explosives. His arm contracted in pain before his hand released the stick, causing it to arc softly and land well in front of its target.

He dropped the rifle from his right hand and switched the dynamite to it, setting his feet firmly and hurling the stick overhand into the mouth of the cave. He bent down for the rifle and again raised it to his shoulder. Within seconds two men came out running. He put the bead on one but did not get off a shot, for they ran directly over the first stick of dynamite just as the flame reached the blasting cap. It exploded, sending pieces of their bodies erupting into the air and raining down bits of blood and bone.

He waited for a while, concealed in the rocks beyond the wagon. There were three horses and three dead men, but caution was a prudent man's friend, so he waited until his concern had dissipated, then walked down the slope for his horse.

He rode over the grounds, reading what he could from the tracks. He walked the horse back and forth around the cave mouth in ever-widening arcs, until he came upon the fresh tracks of three riders headed south along the hillside. He followed them less than a quarter of a mile and stopped. They had not imagined he would cross the bowl and ride directly to them. They intended to stop him along the ridge as they made their way to town. They were taking the long way.

He turned his horse into the bowl and set it to a gallop.

9

The three riders stopped their horses and listened to the reverberations of the explosion ricochet off the hillside and into the bowl. They sat and listened, just as they had sat and listened to the volley of gunfire that had preceded it.

Big Will unclenched his jaw and ran his tongue over his teeth. He'd realized a while back they weren't going to come across Hammond the way they were headed. Still, he had put low odds on the man taking the quick route through open country. Bill and Jody's jabbering over the matter had caused his jaw to seize up, at which point he barked at them to shut up. They did, for a minute. When the shooting began the two men started back up. They were too far along to turn around; the missionary settlement was already in sight. The boys would kill Hammond or Hammond would kill the boys. One or the other.

The dynamite blast put an end to the debate. Big Will could relax. The Cupper brothers and Junior had finished him off and gotten back to work.

'You two gonna shut up about it now?' he growled at them.

'He might still be alive,' said Jody.

'He's not alive you idiot; they've gone back to blasting.'

'Maybe,' said Jody. 'We don't know that though. Seems strange they'd go back to work not half a minute after they shot him.'

Big Will felt his jaw tighten. It did seem strange.

'Shouldn't we go back?' asked Bill. 'Either he's dead and we got work to do, or he still needs killing.'

'No,' said Big Will. 'We're riding to the missionaries.'

'Why? We know he ain't there.'

'Those goddamn missionaries are what brought him here. They find out Hammond's dead and they'll just send for another. This is why I didn't want any of them leaving in the first place.'

'Can we have some fun with the women before we kill 'em?' asked Jody.

'We don't even know if there are any.'

'But saying there is.'

'You've seen the men. You think the women look any better?'

'Maybe they been giving the food to the women. Maybe that's why the men are all so skinny.'

'Do whatever you want,' said Big Will. 'Just make sure they're all dead before we leave.'

They rode down from the hills and into the flatlands of the bowl. Dust stirred beneath the horses' hooves, and when they stopped to observe the missionary settlement away in the distance the dust swirled upwards in a cloud and made them cough.

Two scrawny mules and a half-dead horse stood under the juniper shade in the corral by the dry creek bed. Frank and Donnie's horses stood alongside them. Five wagons sat on the other side of the chicken wire with their tongues dug into the sand. Big Will wondered to himself where the draft animals were at. It occurred to him they had most likely been eaten. What else was there to eat in this spot of hell?

The missionaries had hand-dug a well in the bottom of the dry creek where it was most shaded by the junipers. He rode to it and his men followed. They sent the bucket down half expecting the well to be dry. It came up with water, cool on their throats. They drank and watched the settlement from the shade.

'I don't see nobody,' said Jody after he had taken his drink.

'They're there,' said Big Will.

'Where?'

'Holed up.'

'Which house?'

'Could be any one.'

'How we gonna find out?'

'Will you shut up with the goddamn questions, Jody.'

'I was wondering too,' said Bill. 'Why don't we just ride in and open the doors and shoot 'em?'

'That's why they call us the Jones' gang and not the Bill and Jody gang. You two idiots would go in there and get yourselves shot. You haven't thought they might be sitting inside one of those houses all with guns aimed at the door?'

Bill and Jody didn't answer.

'Just shut up and watch,' said Big Will.

Not but a few minutes went by when the church door opened and a bearded man poked his head out. He glanced about nervously then darted for the privy. When he had stepped inside and closed the door they left the corral in a run. They did not stop and wait upon reaching the privy, but instead flung open the door and pulled the emaciated man off the seat and into the sun.

'Shut your mouth,' Big Will told him, holding his gun to the man's head as he attempted to pull his britches up. 'Answer these questions. Is everyone in that same building you came out of?'

'You mean the church?' the man asked through the beard.

'Whatever it is. You all in there?'

'Yes.'

'Ya'll got guns?'

'No.'

'You lyin' to me?'

'No, I swear.'

'He's lying,' said Jody.

'How many of you are there?'

'Ah, nine, yes nine of us.'

'Nine of you,' Big Will stared the man in the eyes as if to deduce any falsehood in them. 'What's your name?'

'Simon Foster.'

'You got women in there, Simon?' interjected Jody.

'Shutup, Jody,' said Big Will.

'Yes, there's women.'

'There are?'

'Yes.'

'How many?' said Big Will.

'Four women.'

'Four women!' exclaimed Jody. 'Ain't that nice? Four women and three of us. We can throw the ugly one out.'

'Get walking,' said Big Will. He took hold of Simon's shirt collar and pushed him forward, keeping the gun raised at the back of his head.

They reached the church door and Big Will called out in his baritone voice. 'Hey! We got your man Simon Foster out here. Open the door or we shoot him.'

A moment of silence from inside, then a voice called out in response, 'Who is it?'

'It's William Jones. What the hell does it matter? Open the goddamn door.'

'How do we know you have Simon?' came the voice.

Big Will gave Simon a knock on the head with the gun barrel. 'Say something.'

'Reverend Mattick, please, open the door. They have guns. They'll shoot me.'

'Is that you, Simon?' answered the Reverend from inside.

'Yes, please, open the door!'

Silence followed. Big Will stood in the dust before the doorway, one hand still clutched around Simon's collar, the other holding the gun. Bill and Jody stood close behind, their own guns drawn. They waited, expecting to hear the slide of the drawbar behind the door. Nothing came. Big Will glanced behind him at Jody. Jody stared back.

'Open that door!' Big Will shouted again.

No response.

Big Will turned his head to Jody. 'Kick that door in.'

Jody stepped forward and slammed the sole of his boot into the door then spun away hopping on the opposite foot and his face in pain. The door hadn't budged.

'Listen here, Reverend,' said Big Will. 'We're going to kill this man Simon if you don't hurry it up.'

Bill moved up from behind. 'What are they doing in there?' he said, directing the question as much to Simon as to Big Will.

Neither responded.

'Why don't you just shoot him?' whispered Bill.

'We shoot him and they'll never open the door,' said Big Will.

'Well they ain't opening up the door now.'

'Shutup.'

A moment later the Reverend's voice came through again. 'If we give you a woman will you let Simon go and leave us in peace?'

Big Will looked at Bill, then Jody. He thought he had misunderstood the question, but the looks on his men's faces told him he had not.

'What?' he shouted anyway.

'If we give you a woman. Will you let Simon go and let us be?'

Big Will stared at the door. 'Yeah,' he said.

Jody shook his head beside him. 'What?' he mouthed silently.

'Shutup,' hissed Big Will.

Another moment of silence followed and the door opened a crack.

Without hesitating, Big Will shoved Simon into it, knocking the door wide open. He pushed the thin man all the way through and when he had crossed the threshold threw him forward and into the Reverend, who was pushing forward a woman much the way Big Will had ushered in Simon.

They collided and fell to the floor and Big Will stepped over them followed by Bill and Jody. They fanned out, guns drawn. Big Will wasted no time barking orders.

'Stand up you dumb sons of bitches, all of you! Get up. Don't want to open a goddamn door...' he looked them over as he snarled at them, and when his eyes fell on the women he made a face and his voice trailed off. He looked at the one picking herself up from the floor. 'At least you were gonna give us the pretty one,' he said. He gave Bill and Jody a look and motioned to the three other women in the room. 'You can have them too if you want, boys,' he laughed recklessly, eyes wide open. 'You want them old hags?' he could hardly speak he was laughing so hard.

Bill and Jody needlessly negated with a shake of their heads.

'You,' Big Will looked at the woman on the floor. 'Stay over here. The rest of you line up along that wall. Right under that cross behind the pulpit.'

'What are you going to do to us?' Big Will recognized the voice of the Reverend that had spoken through the door.

'I ain't made my mind up about that yet,' he said.

'Will?' interrupted Jody. 'What's that?'

Big Will followed Jody's eyes to the pew. On it sat a glass jar. He walked to it and picked it up and held it in the air and shook it. He looked at the men and women against the wall.

'There must be a pound of gold here. Maybe more,' he tossed it to Bill. 'What do you say Bill?'

'About that. Once you break off the quartz.'

'A pound of gold. How much more you got?'

The eight lined against the wall stared back mutely.

'How much more goddamn gold have you sons of bitches got?' he said flatly.

'That's our gold,' said the Reverend defiantly. 'It's our mine and it's our gold. You men are thieves.'

'We already heard that shit. I believe it was that man right there,' Big Will pointed to Paul, 'who started up with that speech. Paul Conner if I remember correct.

Well, we didn't listen to it all. We gave Paul there a whuppin instead. You fancy catching a beating too, preacher man?'

'I think he does,' said Jody.

'Tell me where it is,' said Big Will.

'It's all of it,' said Reverend Mattick. 'We don't have anymore.'

'Bullshit.'

'I swear to you…'

'How about I start shooting you? One by one. Will that do it? How many of you am I gonna have to go through till somebody tells me where it is, huh?' he pointed his gun at them and flicked it upwards as if recoiling from a blast.

They flinched but none talked. They were hard cases. He wondered if shooting them would get them talking or have the opposite effect. It might just bind them up tighter. These religious folk were hard to figure.

'I say shoot 'em,' said Bill.

Big Will turned around. 'What's your name?' he said to the pretty one.

'Rose.'

'Rose. Tell me where it's at.'

'I don't know. If there is anymore I don't know where it's at. It's the truth.'

'Jody, take Rose here to one of the houses. Maybe you can hump the answer out of her.'

Jody grabbed the woman by the upper arm and pulled her to the church door. He dropped his gun in its holster and swung the door open with his free hand. He pulled her with him, and no sooner had he crossed the doorway than he recoiled backwards, flinging Rose back inside with him. He swung the door closed and spun around.

'It's Hammond!' he blurted.

Big Will ran to the door but hesitated on opening it. 'Did he see you?'

'No. I don't think he did.'

'Bill, you stay here with the missionaries. Any of them make a noise or does something funny, shoot 'em. Jody, get out that window. We'll circle around and shoot that son of a bitch before he knows we're here.'

The two men crawled out the window opposite the street and dropped in the dust outside. They squatted alongside the adobe wall for a minute, listening to nothing but their own breathing before breaking into a run to the nearest house. Along the wall they crept, pausing before reaching the street.

'I don't see him nowhere,' whispered Big Will. 'You sure he didn't see you?'

'I don't think he did.'

'Then where is he?'

Jody only looked wide-eyed at his boss and shook his head weakly.

'Go around to the other side,' said Big Will. 'You come out and we'll have one of us in front of him and one in back.'

Jody turned and disappeared around back of the house. Big Will watched him go. He wasn't sure at all of his plan. He didn't know where on the street Hammond was. But he was impatient. He had gold on the mind. Goddamn missionaries sitting with a pound of it in a glass jar. It made his head throb.

He counted a few more seconds off and walked around the front of the house with his gun drawn.

Hammond's horse stood riderless in the street. Jody appeared on the other side of the house, and Big Will nearly shot him. His nerves were worked up. Goddamn jaw was clenched up again.

The two men walked further into the street. There was no sound, only the sweltering weight of the sun, sending rivulets of sweat beading down their faces in thin trickles. They walked slowly, turning as they moved, ears and eyes strained for input. Big Will could feel his chest tightening. What the hell was happening, he asked himself. How did it occur to him to come out into the street like this?

'Bill!' he shouted suddenly. 'Get out here!'

The church door creaked open and slammed shut. Bill stood on the other side. The movement drew the eyes of Big Will and Jody. They turned back around to the street and Les Hammond was there, gun drawn, and the desert silence was broken by the thunder of gunfire.

Jody took a bullet through the chest and dropped where he had been standing. Big Will fired, pulling the hammer back on the revolver with his free palm and pulling the trigger as fast as the cylinder would spin. He saw Hammond lurch and drop to a knee, and fired into him, even as he felt the thud of bullets pound his body.

Hammond rolled and came to a knee and fired again. Big Will heard Bill scream behind him. Hammond's gun cracked and the screaming stopped and Big Will looked down confused, wondering why he was on his knees. Then his face was in the dirt and he struggled to understand why. He swung a leg around, and his ear rolled onto the ground. His eyes looked sideways onto the street.

Les Hammond staggered towards the church. Blood ran from his skull, down his face and along his shirtfront. Bill rose suddenly from the ground in front of the church, clutching his bloody neck, and fired at Hammond. The bullet kicked up dust fifty yards behind its target and

Hammond's gun responded with a boom that dropped Bill back to the dust.

Hammond limped unsteadily towards him, thumbing rounds into his gun. He reached Bill and looked down a moment, ensuring the man was dead, then turned and opened the church door to the nine horrified faces of the men and women inside. They remained against the wall where they had been instructed to stand; eight skinny bodies all in a row, and Rose standing apart.

He attempted to speak but no words came. The room spun. He took several more steps forward and twisted back around at the sound of the church door creaking open.

Big Will stood in the archway, his face grey and glistening with sweat. Hammond felt the thwack of a bullet hit him, then another, even as his own gun was jerking in his palm. His vision turned opaque and a buzz filled his ears. The only sensation remaining in him was the buck of the revolver as he fired shots into the blurred outline of William Jones. He let go four shots and felt himself fall through space and land heavily on his back. His greyed vision turned darker. Blackness came over him and he lay motionless on the dirt of the church floor, his blood pooling out of him and mixing with the earth beneath.

10

Horrified. That's what we were. I myself found the need to sit on the pew, for my legs shook and I felt faint.

None of us spoke during that first minute as the echoes of gunfire seemed to hold their ring in the hall of our church. The smell of gunsmoke hung in the air, acrid in our nostrils. We stared at them, the men's bodies crumpled on the ground and soiling the floor with their blood. Reverend Mattick was the first to break the silence.

'Is everyone alright?' he asked. 'No one is injured?'

We were. All of us. Thank God.

It was then that Les Hammond moved. He moved an arm and a wheeze escaped his lips. We recoiled, all of us, for we thought surely he was dead. His face was stained dark in blood, and his shirtfront was soaked in it. It continued to seep from his wounds, pooling in a thick puddle on the ground.

We shied away from him. Except for Rose. She ran to him and knelt at his waist, staining her dress in blood. She laid her hands on him, attempting to plug the wounds with her fingers. Blood leaked through them.

'He's still alive,' she said, looking up at us.

I did not know what to say, and neither did the others.

'We have to help him,' she went on. 'He'll die if we don't.'

Her words were prescient. The truth in them connected with us, and I saw several heads nod as she spoke. Yes, he would die. Soon.

'There's nothing we can do, Rose,' said Ruth Mattick. 'You'll only prolong his suffering.'

'Of course there is! We have string, and needles. Every one of us. We can sew his wounds closed. Someone go for them. Sara, you have a bottle of turpentine, do you not? We have bandages-- we used them on Amos when he cut himself last spring. Remember?'

'Rose,' said Reverend Mattick, 'this man is on his way to a better place.'

'But we can help him.'

'Only God can decide whether a man is to live or die.'

'Is no one going to help?' she said.

'Why are you so concerned with this sinner?' said Sara Conner. I felt a lift in my spirit when Sara spoke. Someone had to ask it. 'What do you think he's going to do if we nurse him back to health?'

Rose did not respond. She only looked at us from beside Hammond's bleeding body.

'He's gonna go asking for that money,' said Paul. 'He ain't showed one bit of concern for us. All he wants to know is when he's gonna get paid.'

'It's true,' I said. 'It's all he's talked about since he arrived.'

'We don't have five thousand dollars,' said Simon. 'You've seen how quick he is to kill. What do you think he's going to do to us?'

'I agree,' said his wife. 'He was supposed to be a Good Samaritan, but he's turned out to be nothing but a paid murderer.'

'But you promised it to him,' said Rose. 'He risked his life for us. Look at him. He's dying!'

The Reverend had not spoken. He had listened, as a wise man does, and when he spoke his words held a profound truth to them. 'This man's reward,' he said, 'is not of this earth. It is to sit beside our Lord God in heaven. That is his payment.'

'Amen,' I said.

'Now let him die peacefully. Take your hands from him. Let God's will be done.'

Rose had tears in her eyes. They welled and pooled over her eyelids and ran down her cheeks. 'You people are sick,' she said, looking at each of us. She stood, blood dribbling down the folds of her dress, and left through the church door.

'That woman is reprehensible,' said Sara, when Rose had gone.

'She's probably upset still,' mumbled Vander. 'About the Bible story. Sending her out and all.'

'She wouldn't allow a single thread of her hair to be harmed if it would save us all,' said Sara.

No one denied this. Vander did not respond.

We remained in silence, watching Hammond. Waiting for him to die. His chest continued to rise and fall. He coughed at one point, and I thought it might be the final cry of his soul as it left his body, but it was not. He continued breathing. The bleeding had come to a stop. It made us anxious, all of us.

'Should we do something, Reverend?' asked Paul.

'No, Paul. He will pass soon. When he does we will bury his body with the others and give him a proper service.'

But he did not die. He continued to breathe, and time continued to pass, and all the while the eight of us engrossed by the sight of him, shocked by what the day had brought. By evening the situation had changed little. Hammond slept on the ground, the color drained from his face. We stayed with him as though it were a vigil. Waiting. Watching.

Reverend Mattick chose Simon and Vander to take the three dead men's bodies to the graveyard and bury them there. It was small relief, but relief we would take; having their corpses removed from our sight.

When the sun had set and darkness began to enter the church his condition had not changed. We were tired, exhausted really, by the events of the day, yet the idea of leaving this man alone and unsupervised disquieted us. We discussed our options of who might stay with him, but none of us were eager to volunteer. And the details; how many would need to remain in the church? What if he awoke in a state of confusion or anger? What then?

We considered drawing straws. Four of us could stay awake with Hammond while the rest slept, changing shifts after midnight. But for how long might this go on?

Mary Foster, bless her, led us to the solution. Simon had suggested simply leaving the man in the church unattended, for he was certain Hammond would die before sunrise, but Mary's fear was too great.

'And what if he doesn't?' she asked. 'What if he rises in the night and comes to us demanding his payment? What then?'

We had no answer for her.

'He must stay here,' she said. 'And we must accept that he may not die tonight. How long will we stay awake watching over him? It might be days. How much sleep do you want to lose? No. It won't work.'

'What do you suggest then, Mary?' said her husband. 'We can't very well bar the door from the outside. Nor the windows.'

'Rope,' she said. 'Gather rope from the houses. We'll tie him to the pew.'

And there it was. The answer to our dilemma. An answer inspired by the Holy Spirit no doubt. We had no reason to dither. Paul Conner walked to his house and returned with a coil of plaited rope.

Hammond's moans as we wound the rope in loops over his body gave us shivers. He appeared to gain consciousness at one point. His eyes opened and he looked at me, and I will admit I made a quick prayer to the Lord to strike the man dead right there. But He did not. The Lord tests us all, yet never more than we can bear. We knotted the rope several times around the base of the pew, and not one of us declined to test the tautness of its fibers upon finishing.

Satisfied with our work and ready for bed, we left him alone to die at peace.

As for Rose, I would have to speak with the Reverend. It could not wait much longer.

11

When Vander returned after dark he did not look at her. She stood against the wall with her arms crossed, feeling like an unwelcomed guest in the closest thing she could call her home. She watched him remove his hat and place it on the table, then open the chest where he kept his bottle and rummage around. Only then did he look at her. Distrustfully, as though she might tell. She never did though. There was no point.

She had never had much to say to him. She had tried, at the beginning, but he was a man short on words, if not intellect. He had nothing to say to her. She was something to poke in the night when the liquor sufficiently aroused his urges.

She certainly had no wish to speak to him now. She could barely stand to remain in the room with him. He had said nothing in the church. Not a word of protest. She knew there was no love within him, but had preferred to delude herself with the thought that there might lie some feeling of affection, be it lukewarm or otherwise.

That he would be affected in some way should he lose her. But there was none.

He had sat like a mute, callous, eyes glazed over at the church wall when Mary Foster had brought up the story in the book of Judges. William Jones was at the door, Simon's fate in his hands. Reverend Mattick stood under the cross frozen with indecision.

'Open the door,' Mary had pleaded.

'They'll kill us all if we do,' said Ruth.

'It's my husband!'

'We can't let them enter,' Amos had said.

'Give them the gold. The gold for Simon,' Mary begged.

'No,' said Amos.

'Then give them Rose. They'll take a woman.'

The Reverend looked up at her, intrigued. He held her eyes and she spoke to him directly, pleading her case, knowing it was his decision in the end. And knowing too, that a man's life was more valuable than a woman's. They all knew that. The Reverend's teachings were not ambiguous.

'The book of Judges,' she had said. 'When the wicked men of Gibeah surrounded the good man's house and demanded he open the door...to harm the Levite. They gave them the women instead, did they not?'

'It's true,' Ruth affirmed.

'Is there not a precedent set then?' said Mary.

The Reverend did not speak, only nodded his head discreetly.

'We need Simon,' said Paul. 'He's the only skilled tradesman amongst us. What we will do should a wagon wheel break, or the well cave in?'

The Reverend needed no more argument. He stood and approached the door. 'If we give you a woman will you let Simon go and leave us in peace?' he shouted.

And now Vander sat in his chair with his lips to the bottle and her standing against the wall as though she were nothing. Not a word to her about it.

She could go the rest of her life without interchanging a word with him. She would be happier that way. But in that moment, she needed to know.

'Is he dead?' she said.

'No.'

'He's still alive?'

'Yeah.'

'Is he still in the church?'

Vander looked at her annoyed but didn't answer. He took another drink.

'Did you leave him in the church?' she asked.

'You can quit worrying, he ain't going nowhere.'

'Of course not. He's nearly dead.'

'Better than that. We tied him up.'

'You tied him up?'

'Tied him to the pew. With rope. He ain't going nowhere.'

'You gave him no help then? You just tied him and left him alone to die?'

'You're awfully worried about that man.'

'He's a human being. Look what he did for us.'

'Shut your mouth woman. I'm tired of listening to it.'

'And you people call yourselves righteous.'

'I said shut it.'

'You're disgusting. All of you.'

He lunged drunkenly from the chair, but she was closer to the door. She flew through it in dirty bare feet and ran, less concerned with the spines of cholla that might lay underfoot than she was of her drunk husband.

He gave up quickly; he did not feel like running. She walked to the creekbed a half mile out from the corral and hung her head in her hands but did not cry. She thought of Les Hammond alone and bullet-ridden, tied to the base of the church pew. She thought of her parents, a lifetime ago, and of sitting in church day after day listening to the filth Reverend Mattick spewed. She thought of the dead babies lying along the trail, their bones white against the withered grass.

The moon rose over her and she sat with her knees drawn up to her body, shivering in the cold of night. She could feel the dried blood of Les Hammond caked on her dress. She waited.

When even the great horned owls had ceased to make their calls she rose and walked back. The cold sand shifted beneath her toes and left faint imprints of her passing. She walked through the door of the house and stood for a moment to allow her eyes to adjust to the darker interior. From the butcher block beside the stove she picked up the kitchen knife. She crossed the dirt floor to where Vander's inebriated snores rose and knelt beside him and raised the knife and drove it down.

The blade sliced into the soft flesh of his neck, and she ripped it towards her, slashing the throat open. Vander's hands jerked to his neck and he rolled over, coughing and gurgling and spitting blood onto the blankets.

She jumped up and took several steps backwards. She watched the shaded figure lurch on the floor of the adobe house until he stopped fighting and lay still. She then returned the knife to the butcher block and lit a candle and set it in its holder on the table.

In the same chest where Vander kept his liquor were needle and thread. She dug them out and held the needle over the flame until it nearly glowed. When it was too hot to hold she wrapped it carefully in a cloth. Before blowing out the flame she pulled Vander's last bottle of alcohol from the chest. She grabbed a handful of rags and threw them in a pail along with the candle, needle, thread, and matches, and walked back out into the night.

Darkness never completely settled into the desert night. An endless profundity of stars cast their points of light from far-flung galaxies across the heavens down to earth. They converted the red clay into a mix of violet and maroon; yanking it from the emptiness of blackness and casting it onto the edge of color. The stars gave outline to all things physical.

Rose stood along the wall at the edge of her house, watching for movement under the blanket of starlight above her. Nothing stirred. She walked quickly to the church but did not run.

Hammond lay asleep in the dirt, his body tight against the pew. His breath rolled over in even rhythm.

It took her a quarter of an hour to untie the rope. The light from the candle flickered weakly, forcing her to bring her eyes close to her work and squint as she fought with the knots of plaited rope. When he was free she unbuttoned his shirt front and pulled his trousers off.

She started at his head. A bullet had grazed his skull stretching five inches from his temple. It left an open gash, which she dabbed with a rag soaked in alcohol. He jerked when she placed it to his head. His eyes opened and he let out a gasp. She hushed him, and his eyes closed as quickly as they had opened.

Another bullet had struck him between the neck and shoulder, exiting completely. He woke again when she pierced his skin with the needle. His hand shot up and gripped her arm, and he held it tightly while she hushed him and whispered soothing words. The realization came to him that she was helping, and he released her arm and watched her thin frame as she worked by candlelight.

She sewed closed the bullet holes and continued to work her way down his body. Another bullet had struck the edge of his chest. It had glanced off a rib and lodged itself in the meat of the latissimus dorsi. He had taken two more bullets both in the left leg. Both had gone through, and it was from these holes he had bled the most. She re-threaded the needle and began to weave the thread through the skin, closing the holes tight and tying off the thread in small knots. She bathed the wounds in alcohol when she had finished, then returned to the bullet lodged along his ribs. It was right along the skin; she could feel it with her fingers.

She blew out the candle and left him there to return to her house, this time in a run. She took a paring knife from the kitchen and another pail, and instead of returning directly to the church, went first to the well and drew a pail of water.

Hammond had not moved from where she left him.

She re-lit the candle and heated the blade of the paring knife in it. The skin was stretched tight over the bullet; it was that close to the surface. He gasped when she cut him, and she covered his mouth with a hand. The bullet came out wet and slimy, covered in blood. She dropped it in the pocket of her dress and went back to work with the needle and thread.

When she had finished she went over his body once more, moving the candle along his extremities, looking for wounds. She found only one; a gash in his arm where the tricep blended into the shoulder. There was no time to stitch it shut. Dawn would break soon, and retying the knots would take time.

She cleaned the bullet wounds with rags and water and applied another coat of alcohol before she redressed him. She gave him water and he drank slowly, his eyes looking at her, too weak to talk.

Doubt came over her for a moment. She would have liked to take him away from there and back to her house. He would never make it. He was too weak to walk and too heavy to carry. Time is what he needed. Time to recover or time to die, and if he died her hopes would die with him.

He did not protest when she wound the rope around his body and tied him to the pew. He might have, had he had the strength to speak.

12

Les Hammond lay in the dirt, hugged tight against the pew. There was no cause for struggle; he was too weak to do anything even if he were to escape the rope. The morning light had begun to seep into the church through the windows and as it did the events leading to his condition began to align themselves in his mind. His memories filed themselves into chronological order and he watched them play across his vision.

He felt something was missing. He remembered the shooter in the bowl and the dynamite blast that had killed the two in the cave. He remembered the shootout with Big Will and his men. He remembered stumbling into the church and turning at the sound of the door. He remembered the feel of bullets pounding into his body.

After that his memory turned nebulous. He thought he had killed Big Will. But who had tied him? And the woman last night who sewed his wounds closed? The same one who had shaken her head at him the day before, he was sure of it. As if to warn him.

His head throbbed. The energy required to analyze such questions drained him and he closed his eyes again.

He did not open them at the sound of people entering the church. He heard their footsteps near him, felt their presence.

'Is he still alive?' a voice questioned.

'He's breathing,' came Reverend Mattick's voice.

'It won't be long. Just look how much blood he lost.'

'Should we take his gun away?' a woman's voice asked.

'I don't want to touch it,' said another.

'Leave him,' said the Reverend. 'He'll be dead soon.'

'How are we to hold service today?' Hammond recognized the voice of Amos Dowdry. 'Surely none of us will be able to concentrate with this man lying here.'

'We will hold service, Amos,' said the Reverend. 'A funeral service.'

'Where are Vander and Rose?' asked a woman.

'This is not the first time they have come late to service,' said Amos. 'I've been telling you Reverend…'

'Yes, Amos, I know.'

The creak of the door sounded and it swung shut again.

'Good morning, Rose.'

'Good morning, Reverend.'

'Where is Vander?'

'He's taken ill.'

'Is it serious?'

'No, I'm sure he'll recover soon.'

'We shall pray for him, worry not.'

There was rustling. People moved, they stood still. Reverend Mattick read several bible verses and lead the group in song. Their voices were flat and tired, the notes sung in different keys on varying scales. Hammond dared not open his eyes. The Reverend spoke again. It began as a funeral service, with vague references to a spiritual afterlife. He spoke of the joys in heaven, but soon turned to the sins of mankind. His sermon outlined the return of Christ and the punishment that would befall the unrighteous. He spoke of lukewarm Christians and Laodiceans. He spent a great deal of time describing the horrific torture waiting for them in the Lake of Fire. He outlined their misery with relish, his voice passionate and by the sound of it on the verge of tears. The list of sins he outlined of the inhabitants of Bildsburg, which Hammond could not place, was long enough and depraved enough that he could only imagine it was a biblical reference of which he was unfamiliar.

They sang again, in broken tones, and Reverend Mattick prayed for Hammond's death. They chanted *amen* in unison and exited the church and Hammond opened his eyes and stared at his bare surroundings. He struggled at the ropes but was left weary. He licked his lips and wished for water and closed his eyes.

The congregation returned in the afternoon. The same broken hymns. More bible verses. Descriptions of sin and death and otherworldly vengeance. He closed his eyes tightly and did not open them.

When their service ended they stood around him. He could feel their eyes looking down on him.

'He does not want to leave this earth,' said one.

'It's always the most brutish that cling to life the longest,' said Amos.

'He will surely be dead by morning,' said Reverend Mattick. 'Come brethren. Time to tend to your chores.'

They left him, at which point he slept. He dreamt of the Reverend's words; haunting nightmares intermingled with the faces of the Jones gang. His friend Carl calling out to him.

He woke in the night with the woman beside him. She brought broth to his lips and he drank. It was thin, but in it he tasted salt and stock from bones.

'Can you walk?' she said.

'Yes.'

She brought her candle to the rope and worked at the knots. He watched her, how her hair fell over her shoulders and down her dress.

'Who are these people?' he said.

She paused on the knots and turned her head to him. 'They are people we need to get away from.'

'Who are you?'

'My name is Rose.'

She unstripped the last knot and began to unwind the rope from around his legs. She worked upwards, and when she jerked it from under his back his body flinched and he winced in pain.

'Take my hand,' she said.

He took her hand in his and she pulled firmly on it. His shoulders rose from the floor and a rush came up through his throat and into his skull and clouded his sight. Dizziness swept over him and his hand lost its grip. He fell back to the floor.

When he opened his eyes he felt as though time had passed. It had; his shirt was open and Rose was bent over him, going over the wounds with a wet rag. She placed a bundle beneath his head to prop it up and gave him the broth. He drank slowly but steadily, sipping the liquid down his throat.

'I'll have to tie you again,' she said.

He sipped the broth.

'I don't see infection. The dry desert air is good for you.' She took an end of rope and began to tie him and he stopped her.

'Wait,' he said. 'Take my gun from its holster. There's bullets in the loop on my belt. Reload it.'

She drew it from the holster and held it delicately, unsure of what to do.

'Flip open the loading gate,' he said. 'Draw that hammer back. One more click. See how the cylinder spins now? Drop those rounds into them.'

She slid the cartridges from his belt loop and loaded them one by one into the Colt.

'Hold that hammer back firm and squeeze the trigger. Now let it back down real slow. Put it back in the holster. When you tie me allow my arm some slack, and do not tie the rope over the holster.'

She carried out the instructions without a word. He had questions for her, so many that they ran together in his already aching head. The answers to them were of no use. There was only one question to which the answer was pertinent; when would he regain the strength to move. The woman would not have the answer.

She placed a hand on his shoulder before leaving him.

When he woke it was morning. The church door opened and panic seeped through his system as if replacing the blood that ran through his veins. He felt the faint vibrations of footsteps nearing him.

'He's breathing,' said Amos.

'Perhaps God is deliberating on the fate of his soul,' replied the Reverend.

'I'll tell you the truth, Reverend, I wish he would die.'

'There is no doubt he will, Amos, but you must have patience. The Lord works on His own time.'

'Our own time passes quickly, Reverend.'

'Yes it does.'

'And we cannot regain it.'

'No.'

'Which is why I must speak to you again about Rose.'

'You've already spoken your mind.'

'That was some time ago. Nothing has changed. She is out of control. Storming out of the church the other day. Unrepentant. She is out of place. She needs the firm hand of a man to teach her where she stands. Vander is unable to do so.'

'He is not well. He has not been well for some time I suspect. He has lost the color to his face and seems in a constant state of sluggishness. Rose told me today he will not be attending service.'

'I would make a better husband to her. She would learn to obey me. I would never tolerate such disrespect.'

'I am sure you would not, Amos.'

'Consider her for me, Reverend. No matter Vander's condition.'

'I shall, Amos. You have always been a loyal disciple. I will ensure you are rewarded. And you are right; Rose needs a firm hand. She must be taught to obey her husband, for a woman's place is to serve man, and man's place is to serve God. It is true; Vander has shown that he cannot control her. I have nearly lost patience with him. If he does not show some strength with her soon, I will give her to you.'

'Amen.'

'But do not wish ill on Vander. He is sick. If he is not well by tomorrow we shall visit him and lay hands on him. He is still one of us, Amos, and it will be hard on him further to take his woman from him to give to another man.'

'Yes, Reverend.'

'Now let us tend to our chores before service begins.'

They left the church and Hammond opened his eyes. He felt better. His head was clearer. He stretched his arm down and felt the butt of the gun on his fingers.

The eight men and women entered the church before noon. The service proceeded in much the same way as the day before. Hymns, sermon, more hymns. A prayer for Hammond's death. A break, then another service. A message on the temptations of the devil accompanied by a long-winded and detailed description of the tortures of hell. They sang again to conclude the service, but did not leave.

He could sense them close to him, staring at his body.

'Hard for me to concentrate on the service, Reverend, with this man still lying here alive.'

'Yes, Simon. It's hard for us all.'

'Why has the Lord not taken him?'

'No one understands the mind of God. He works in mysterious ways.'

'Well it bothers me. Bothers my wife too.'

'Is that so, Mary?' asked the Reverend.

'Yes, Reverend. I don't like it. I don't want to see him anymore.'

'I was thinking, Reverend.'

'Yes, Paul?'

'Seems like we could help him along. You know?'

'In what way?'

'Well, he's suffering. You can see it. So wouldn't it be a kind thing for us to do to help him move along to heaven? Seems a Christian like thing to do-- ease his suffering.'

'What do you suggest?'

'Oh, I don't know. Just maybe... stop his breath. He's about dead anyway.'

'As a favor,' joined in Simon.

'It would ease his suffering,' said Mary. 'Why prolong his death?'

'It is kind of you to think this way,' said Reverend Mattick. 'A fine question you ask, Mary; why prolong his death?'

'Let's send him to heaven!' cried Paul.

'That's right,' said Simon. 'Send the man on already. No need to have him suffer here on earth.'

'Place a rag over his mouth,' said Amos. 'It will only take but a minute.'

'Are you all in favor?' asked the Reverend.

A chorus of agreement sounded.

Les Hammond's fingers rested inches from the butt of his Colt. He could feel his heart thump in his chest, could feel his breathing coming faster. He wanted desperately to swallow. He fought the urge. With one motion he could grab the gun and have it in his hand.

But no more had the notion taken root than the doubts seeped in. He had six bullets. There were seven to kill. And he would never get them all. He might kill one or two, but they would move aside, and with the rope restricting his movement he would not be able to reach them.

'We can do it right now,' said Mary. 'We can use the pulpit scarf.' She walked to the pulpit and pulled the fabric cover from it.

'Would you carry out the act, Paul?' asked the Reverend.

'Well I thought--if anyone wants to…Mary has the cloth.'

'I think a man should do it,' said Mary.

'Amos, will you do it?'

'I thought you would, Reverend.'

'Wait,' Rose's voice called out. 'Can we not wait just one more day? Surely he will pass away in the night. He has gone a long while without food or drink. It will be more peaceful in the night.'

'Why is she so eager to keep this man alive?' asked Sara to the congregation.

'It's true,' said the Reverend's wife. 'She wanted to help mend his wounds, remember?'

'If he is not dead by morning I will place the cloth over his mouth and end his life myself,' said Rose. Her voice was strong. It's intention was unwavering.

'Do we all agree to this?' asked the Reverend.

There was a pause, a hesitation of doubt, but no one else would volunteer as executioner. They consented, each of them, and left him on the floor against the pew.

Hours later the sunlight left the church and he lay in darkness.

He found sleep impossible to come by. He waited, staring into the pew and feeling his breath fill him and leave him. He wondered if she would come for him again. Time stretched on. He felt rage and fear, but above all helplessness. He struggled to move his arms, to free himself from the rope, but he could not.

It was at the darkest hour of night she came for him. The door creaked open and his neck strained towards it, fearful that it might be the Reverend or some other madman coming to snuff out his life as he lay helplessly bound by rope.

She knelt at his side in the same manner as the nights previous and lit the candle and looked into his eyes. 'You have no choice this time. Summon the strength.'

'Untie me,' he said.

She took the knots in her fingers and began to unwind them. She unlooped the coils of plaited rope from his ankles, his legs, from around his arms, and threw them aside, then blew out the candle. She leaned low for his arm to find support across her shoulders and they stood as one. They paused, the two of them testing the bounds of balance, his arm across her shoulder and hers around his waist.

Outside the church it was brighter than he had expected. He could clearly see the five adobe houses, and in the distance the shadows of the junipers lining the creek bed. Lit by the moon, all of it.

Once he stumbled but did not fall. They reached the house and he dropped to the ground by the kitchen table. He rolled to his back while she lit a candle.

He smelled it first. The smell of blood, of decaying flesh. It smelled of a butcher shop. The flame took on the candlewick and flickered against the adobe walls. Vander's body appeared out of the darkness. His face was grey and swollen in the candlelight, dark spots of blood splatter covering his chin and chest.

'Who is that?' said Hammond.

'That was my husband,' said Rose.

'What happened to him?'

'I killed him with a knife.'

He turned to look at her from his supine position on the floor. She walked to the body and took a blanket from the ground and draped it over his torso and head.

'What do you plan to do to me?' said Hammond.

'I plan to give you more broth and some solid food if you can take it. I'll clean your wounds and when you are strong again you will take your gun and kill every last one of them. I have no money and cannot pretend to pay you. But there is the mine. It is real, the gold is there, and you can have all that you can dig out. I ask for none of it. Just promise me when you leave here you will take me with you. Far from here.'

She held the candle in front of her. The glow it cast threw shadows over her face from below. It accentuated the fullness of her lips and dipped into the hollow of her cheeks, long without adequate sustenance.

Les Hammond nodded. 'I don't need anymore than what I asked for. Figuring we make it out of here alive, anything beyond my five thousand is yours. That's if they don't find us first. And that's why I can't stay here.'

'There is nowhere to go. Besides, you're too weak. You can hardly walk.'

'I can't stay here,' he said again. Yet even as the words left his mouth he felt blackness coming over him, eyes fogging over. 'Where's my horse?'

'In the corral.'

'And the Jones's horses?'

'Also in the corral. Except for the one they slaughtered.'

'What?'

'We have no food. We've eaten most of the animals already. When we first arrived here a year ago the rains had filled the creek and there was life and vegetation. Now there is nothing. Nothing to eat. No crops. We thought the rains would start a month ago, but there's been nothing.'

'The rains will come soon. You can feel it in the air.'

'You think so?'

'It'll come, and when it does it'll come heavy.'

She watched him unbutton his shirt and inspect the stitches.

'Can any of these boys track?' he asked.

'No.'

'Saddle my horse and bring him here.'

'Where will you go?'

'To the mine. The Jones's left food and water. There's shelter.'

'How will you ever make it? Shouldn't you stay here?' Her voice choked and the undersides of her eyes tightened as tears welled in them. 'Are you going to leave me?' she said.

'I promise you I will not leave you. I will come back. But tomorrow they'll be looking for me. I can't be here.'

She stood in the candlelight, her eyes fixed upon him. She held his eyes in hers and felt the beat of her heart in her chest. 'Alright,' she said, and turned and left through the doorway. When she returned he was propped on one elbow with his revolver disassembled. He asked for a rag which he ran through the barrel and each chamber of the cylinder, then wiped the residue of gunpowder off the cylinder base.

As he worked on the gun Rose took Vander's canteen from the wall and filled it with bone stock. She took her own blanket from the floor and when Hammond was ready she helped him outside and into the saddle, and passed him the blanket and canteen.

They exchanged no words, only a look between them.

Away from her he rode. Away from the town and into the open expanse of the desert bowl, an infinity of constellations overhead.

13

There are no words to describe the terror that befell me when we opened the church door and saw the plaited rope lying unwound in unordered coils beside the pew. I took hold of Reverend Mattick's shoulder, so near I was to falling faint. We entered slowly, cautiously, taking the rope in our hands and staring perplexed and befuddled and without answer.

'Remain strong, Amos,' said the Reverend. 'We must call in the brethren. Quickly.'

We ran to the houses, pounding the doors with our fists and shouting for them to gather in the church. They came running, shortly rising from their beds and still dressed in their nightgowns. They covered their mouths at the sight of the empty ropes and looked over their shoulders in fright as though the man might be just behind them.

Confusion ran without restraint. The brethren spoke at once; theories and accusations. Who had tied the rope? Why had we not checked that the knots were secure?

Reverend Mattick hushed them. 'Is everyone ok? Where is Vander?'

We looked at Rose together as one. She stood aloof in the corner, unperturbed I would almost say if I didn't know better.

'Paul, Simon, go fetch him. No one can remain alone.'

'He is--,' said Rose, 'he is at the mine.'

'What do you mean?' said the Reverend.

'He woke early this morning and his affliction had left him. He felt very much refreshed. He wanted to begin work on the mine-- to make up for not taking part in the butchering yesterday.'

'I did not see him,' I said, 'and I have been awake since dawn.'

'He left early, before the sun rose.'

'He's in danger then,' Ruth blurted.

'Calm yourself,' said the Reverend. 'Everyone remain calm. Let us understand the situation first. The man is gone. What of his horse? Is his horse gone?'

Paul made to open the door, but paused, the thought I am sure occurring to him that the murderer might be on the other side. But he was not, of course. We filed back into the street, needing only a few steps to see around to the corral. His horse was gone. We looked about our surroundings again, seeing the man in every shadow and behind every wall.

But he was nowhere. It took us some time to understand this. We walked in a tight group, convincing ourselves there was safety in numbers. We covered the town that way.

And just like that he was gone. Relief swarmed over us in a wave of ecstasy as we came to the realization that we were free of the Jones's and free of Les Hammond and delivered out of evil and into good fortune by the hands of God.

Reverend Mattick gave a prayer right there in the street with the seven of us gathered round. He gave thanks and praise, vowing to live by His law and supplicating to His Holiness that we should never lay eyes upon Les Hammond again.

I tell you it was freedom. Like innocent captives released from the confines of a prison cell. We smiled and laughed, and found merriment in the sight of alleviation upon each other's faces. And to add to our joy it was not only myself, but several of us that had heard the cracks of thunder late in the night, far to the north. Soon the rains would come. Our famine would be ended.

No sooner had we begun to celebrate our freedom, and the promise of the summer rains, than we found our minds turning to the gold. So long it had been since we had gone to the cave to work the mine. It was all there for us now, waiting.

We needed direction and order, which is precisely what Reverend Mattick gave us.

'Paul, Simon,' he said, 'hitch the mules to the wagon and load what supplies you might need. Mary, Sara, fill a barrel with water and go with them. Our time has come, brethren. There is no limit to what God has in store for us.'

They returned to their houses to change into proper clothing and ready themselves for the day. Reverend Mattick went to the church to prepare for the following service. I was already dressed. I walked in a near daze. I felt filled with the power of Christ; strong and eager to conquer what lay before me. I walked amongst the houses, and as I approached the Davidsdottir's I slowed my walk. The shutters on the window were slightly ajar and I paused.

Do not let your mind wander to impure thoughts. I often took walks outside. They helped me find tranquility in nature. Sometimes on these walks I would look in a window; it is only natural. In the Davidsdottir's I would look quite frequently. But with good intentions only. I knew Vander found it difficult to walk the righteous path, and it is a good Christian man who looks out for his brother in Christ. This was my only intention; that if I saw something outside of the guidelines of the Good Book that I might report it to the Reverend. If it so happened that I peered in and Rose was in the midst of changing her garments, or drying herself with a towel after bathing, it was purely coincidental.

It just so happened that as I walked past her house and quietly eased the shutters open a touch more, she was changing from her nightgown and into her dress for the day. Such a sinful figure her soul had been given in the form of flesh. As I watched her undress I felt the power of God surge within me, and knew it was a sign from Him that she must be with me. God would deliver her to me, and I would show her what it meant to serve a man. In every way.

So enticing are the attributes of a woman's body on a helpless man such as I, that the shape of a man lying on the floor nearly escaped me. I tore my eyes from her figure and looked into the shadowed recesses of the corner. There was no mistaking it; the figure of a man lying on the ground, covered with a blanket to hide him. His two legs stuck out from below, and I pulled away from the window and felt the blood rush from my face as the understanding of what had transpired struck me.

I told you that you should not trust her-- that there is wickedness within her. How she must have yearned for Vander to recuperate. I do not believe it was his idea at all to leave for the mine. She had pressured him into it no doubt. Go to the mine Vander, she would have said, go now, for you have lain sick for days and owe it to the congregation to make up for your absence. And no sooner did he depart than she had run to the church and brought the man back to nurse him to health. We should have known. Such eagerness she had displayed to help the man. But the wicked often pull the cloth over the eyes of the holy.

I ran to the church. The features of my face were pulled tight with distress, enough so that Reverend Mattick sprang backwards when I threw open the door and ran to him in gasps of panicked breath. I told him everything I had seen. I cannot remember the words I used, I know they were confusing to the Reverend for he urged me several times to calm myself, to take a breath. My words came so quickly it seemed I was speaking in tongues.

Reverend Mattick could scarce believe it. We exited the church together and crept silently past the Foster's house and alongside the wall of the Davidsdottir's. One look through the open shutter was enough. The Reverend grabbed me and pulled me backwards, and we ran to the street and put distance between the house and ourselves. The time to make decisions was short. Paul and Simon had hitched and loaded the wagon. Mary and Sara sat on the driving seat. Simon and Paul had saddled two of the healthy horses left by William Jones and his men. The mules leaned hard into their collars, turning the wagon wheels slowly across the hard baked clay.

We ran down the street and into the desert after them. We dared not yell, for we could not risk raising Rose's suspicions. We caught them, Reverend Mattick's face resembling what my own must have looked like only minutes before.

They were aghast at our findings. Had it not been for both of us laying eyes on the man they would not have believed it could be true. But then again, it was Rose. And not one of us was unaware of her weak vocation. The women, especially, had sensed her weakness. They had no doubt how easily she could be lead by the Devil into sin. They were quick to point it out.

The Reverend quieted them, thank God. Rose could be dealt with. Our problem was finding a solution to Hammond. He must be killed, there was no disagreement in that respect. But who was to carry out the deed? And how? Not one of us felt comfortable with a gun, much less barging into Vander's house and facing Hammond head-on.

But surely you understand by now the genius of the Reverend. How fluidly he receives the messages of the

Lord. The answer was given to him and he related it to us, and as one we knew it was the answer.

The four would ride on to the mine. Paul would ride back immediately, this time with several sticks of dynamite in his possession. Until he returned, Reverend Mattick, his wife, and myself would keep watch over the house. Our confidence in the use of weapons was short, but of the dynamite we had no doubt. We would cast Hammond from this earth and God and the devil could argue over the fate of his soul.

They put the whip to the mule's shoulders and left us, this time riding with purpose. When the dust had settled I turned to the Reverend.

'And Rose? What shall we do with her?'

'I am undecided.'

'Is this not enough, Reverend? Give her to me. Make her my wife and I will see to it she pays dearly. I will make a proper woman of her, believe my words.'

'I know you will, Amos. And Vander? What of him?'

I shook my head. I did not have the answer. To hell with Vander, I thought to myself. But I could not control my thoughts; Rose consumed them.

How I wanted that woman. By God, I wanted her.

14

Just once Les Hammond nearly passed out in the saddle. He might have, had it not been for the thunder cracks splitting the sky apart and jolting him back from the edge of consciousness. Rain was coming, and soon. He let the horse have the lead, as it seemed to know where it was headed anyway.

The first half of the trail had been easier than he had hoped for. The last mile his head began to spin. By the time the horse walked up within sight of the Jones's wagon he was clutching the saddle horn and fighting to keep his eyes open. He felt the blanket Rose had given him fall from his shoulders, and when he tried for a drink from the canteen it slipped through his fingers and fell to the dirt.

He made no attempt to retrieve them. He fell from the horse and it walked off in search of water. He crawled the remaining distance to the tarp staked down off the wagon's sideboards. He stretched himself out against the tarp where it came slanted down and staked to the ground. Sleep took hold of him like a wolf's bite into the neck of its prey.

The light of morning did not wake him. The voices did. Thirty yards away at the mouth of the cave.

'Lord Jesus,' Hammond recognized the voice of Simon. 'Paul, look at this. This man's been blown to bits.'

'There ain't much left of him.'

'I thought that was thunder woke me up last night.'

'Where's Vander?'

'Simon!' a woman's voice cut through their exchange. Hammond heard no other words. He waited. He heard the sound of boots over loose stone.

'You recognize that, Paul?'

'That's Vander's. I know it well enough, I've drunk from it several times. That's his blanket too. Or maybe Rose's. Either way I've seen him with it.'

'How would that man have known to come up here after Vander?'

'Rose sent him,' the woman's hoarse whisper barely reached Hammond.

'I wouldn't doubt that she did,' said Paul.

'She knew her husband would be here alone. You've all seen how she looks at him with such contempt. She's wicked! I hope Reverend Mattick keeps her locked in that house and blows them both to hell!'

'Sara you know that ain't gonna happen. The Reverend is gonna give her to Amos. Amos needs a woman.'

The other man made a sound. Not a word, but more akin to an audible shudder. There was a pause in the conversation.

'That's fine by me,' said Sara. 'She'll get her time in hell, but let Amos give her a little taste of it first. Paul, don't waste any more time here. Take the dynamite and get back to town. Tell the Reverend what's happened.'

Footsteps compacted the loose gravel. The soft crunch of footfalls came up from the cave and along the side of the tarp, inches from Hammond's body. They turned and continued past his head and stopped at the wagon where the sound of wood scraping against wood told Hammond the box of dynamite had been found.

Hammond could see the man's waist. He saw it twist slightly and the arms come down with sticks of dynamite in each hand.

'May God's hand guide you,' he heard Simon say. Then the creak of a saddle and the horse's hooves compacting the gravel more succinctly than the man's boots.

Hammond pulled the Colt from its holster and lay motionless on his back. He stared at the tarp and thought of where his horse might have gone to. He should have woken earlier. He should have woken with the sun but the heavy clouds had dimmed its light and he had slept as if with urgency.

He heard the man speaking with the two women thirty yards from his feet and wondered how long it would take for them to find him. He pulled the hammer back on the Colt.

It did not take long. The man told one of the women to find what buckets or pails might be in the wagon. She approached the base of the tarp but instead of circling around to the wagon she pulled up short and took several steps backwards towards the cave. They kept their voices low. Only the sound of boots over gravel, quickly at first, slowing as they neared the woman. The boots stopped and what words were spoken did not reach Hammond.

The feet approached him. Two sets; the man first, the woman close behind. They edged toward him, slower as they covered the last few feet. They stopped at the edge where the stakes had been hammered into the ground. Inches from Hammond. He lay still, eyes wide on the tarp next to his face. The sand shifted under the man's feet outside and Hammond rolled towards the wagon wheels.

The sharp metal of a pickaxe tore through the fabric and bit hard into the gravel where Hammond had lain. He came to his knees and shot out the opening by the wheels and turned to see a woman's skeleton face braced as if in pain, her arms swinging a shovel around to his head. He dropped to a knee and his Colt came up and he shot her through the chest as the shovel whiffed over his head. The bearded man behind her brought his pickaxe back up over his head, and before his muscles could contract for a downward blow a bullet exploded from Hammond's gun and smashed into his upper teeth, driving them back through his brain and out the back of his head. The pickaxe dropped from the man's extended arms and he sank to his knees and fell over dead.

Hammond had not forgotten the third woman. He pivoted on a knee toward the cave where she stood with a match to the dynamite. Her right arm arched backwards to throw the lit explosive and he shot her before she could release it. The bullet caught her in her left shoulder, spinning her to the ground. She turned and rose again, her right hand swinging back in an underhand motion and Hammond levered the hammer back once more and felt the buck of the gun as he pulled the trigger and sent another bullet exploding into her chest. He fired again as she fell and saw her body lurch, then ran behind the wagon and ducked before the wick burned to the hilt and sent a blast rocking the hillside into smoke and dust.

When the debris had settled and the hillside returned to its former calm, Hammond reloaded his gun.

He flung open the boxes and bags in the Jones's wagon and found a satchel of beef jerky. He stuffed a piece in his mouth, then let open the spigot on the water barrel and put his mouth under it.

It took a half hour of searching to find his horse. In that time the sky darkened further and claps of thunder rang out close by in the northern sky. He filled a pail with water and let the horse drink, then mounted him and rode down the slope and into the bowl as the first drops of water landed coldly on his shoulders.

15

We needed Rose away from the house and out of sight from it. Reverend Mattick had the answer. Not only to keep her occupied and unable to interfere, but a task too long delayed by us and in need of doing. Months ago we had carved out clay from the creek bottom and formed bricks of adobe with what straw remained. We had planned to build an annex to the church, and though in hindsight the straw we used in the process would have been put to good use feeding the animals, its role in forming bricks to further the house of God had no higher calling.

They were heavy, each one of them, and with the sky clouding over and the rains imminent, it was of urgent importance that they be stored in the church interior. It kept her on the far side of town. The Foster's house blocked her view of us where we waited crouched in the shadows, all eyes on the door behind which Hammond rested.

I questioned if my nerves would withstand it. The Reverend gave himself, his wife and me each a gun taken from the Jones's. We took positions several yards apart from one another and kept our weapons aimed at the Davidsdottir's door. I trembled at the thought of the man rising and walking into the light of day. I prayed to God I would have the strength to shoot him dead.

For the first time in many months I did not sweat during the day. I shivered instead. The sky had darkened and thunderclaps rang out in long booming echoes from the north. A wind began to blow. It picked up the sand of the desert and cast it against the walls of our houses, into our faces and on our clothing.

When Paul arrived racing on a hard-ridden horse it was downright cold. He dropped from the saddle and ran to us, the dynamite clutched in his hand. The wind whipped at his clothing and parted his beard in two.

As if my nerves were not already overwhelmed by our situation, he told us of what they had found at the mine. Vander's body, blown into shards of bone. His blood spewed onto the ground in all directions. The canteen and blanket left behind; the only signs of his passing.

None of us had suspected that Hammond had possessed the strength to ride to the mine and return the very same night. It made sense that he had not moved all day, for surely his body was spent from the effort. It also made clear his intentions for us.

As Paul recounted the details of his findings and clarity took hold on all aspects of our situation, my own future, and that of Rose's, took form. The Reverend and I exchanged a look, and I knew his thoughts and mine were one.

Not a moment was wasted. We lit the wicks and let them burn close to the base of the explosive, all the while walking towards the house, all four of us into the wind. We cast open the shutters and flung inside the instruments of his death before turning and running from the impending blast.

The Lord's own roar of victory I tell you. That is the sound it made. A tremendous thunder outstripping anything the storms of nature could muster. Bits of clay and adobe rained from the sky and I covered my head and did not stop running until the reverberations of deafening sound had subsided and nothing remained of the Davidsdottir's house but rubble and the blood and bone of Les Hammond.

Rose came running. Fear and confusion were streaked across her face, for surely she had realized that her plans were laid bare.

The Reverend grabbed hold of her before she reached the house. She twisted in his arms and I ran to help him. I grabbed hold of her arm, the first time I had laid hands on the woman, and what sweet prelude that first touch was knowing what would soon be mine. The Reverend told her to be silent but she would not stop her screaming.

'What have you done?' she shrieked. 'Why have you done this? My house…'

'He's dead!' I shouted at her gleefully. 'Your husband as well, I am sure you're quite happy.'

'Who is dead?' she asked.

'That vile man who led you to sin, you wicked woman. Blown apart now,' I admonished her.

'But what…why have you--'

'He might have killed Vander, relish your success there, but the righteous can only be fooled for so long. You thought you could hide Hammond from us? You were wrong. The eyes of God are everywhere.'

'Let me go!' she screamed.

The Reverend demanded silence from her yet still she ran her tongue. He brought a hand to her face and slapped it, and I felt called to do the same. How good it felt to strike the insolent wench. A taste of what was to come. A lesson, saying know this; a woman's place is to fear man, as it is man's place to fear God.

We took her to the church and threw her inside and I supplicated to the Reverend that we should be married that very day. He acquiesced, understanding both how long I had waited as well as the length of depravity to which Rose had resorted.

I would have liked to have him run through the nuptial then and there. But Reverend Mattick insisted there must be at least two witnesses present.

'What of Ruth and Paul?' I asked. 'Have them come now.'

The Reverend shook his head. 'So eager you are, Amos. Patience, brother. Would it not be better to wait for Simon, Mary and Sara? Surely they will want to bear witness.'

'With the ferocity of the storm they may decide to spend the night at the mine,' I countered.

'They very well might.'

'The wind is something fierce, and it would be quite dangerous to ride through the bowl if lighting is present.'

Reverend Mattick peered out the window at the blackening sky. 'Good things come to those who wait, do they not, Amos?'

'Yes, Reverend.'

'If they do not return I should go and close their shutters so their houses are not filled with rain. And you must prepare your vows. Take your time with them. I will return shortly. If Simon and the women have not come back we will marry you with only Paul and my wife as witnesses.'

'Very well, Reverend. Thank you,' I said.

He bowed his head slightly. Before he left he gave a stern look to Rose, standing still with her arms crossed in the corner.

I shut the door behind him and took from the pulpit a piece of paper and the Reverend's fountain pen. Seated in the pew I found it hard to concentrate on my vows. Rose paced back and forth, and it did occur to me she might run out the door. You know how women can become hysterical. I rose and let the drawbar drop into the racking. Should she decide to attempt an escape it would cost her extra time. I had no cause to worry though; she knew there was nowhere to run to. She was a wicked woman in need of taming, but not a fool.

She did not speak to me. Not once. She only stood there in the corner with her arms crossed and such a look of disobedience across her face I near gave her another taste of my palm. But I did not. I am not a rash man. I composed myself and set to work on my vows.

Clouds continued to build outside. The rain had only started to sprinkle, but suddenly it came with a crash. The wind swept it into the church and I ran to close the shutters. My papers were blown about and I scooped them up in the dark and found it necessary to light a row of votive candles to see by, though it was not yet dusk.

There was no chance Simon would return with the the women. Not with the tempest such as it was. And I was correct. The Reverend returned with the same understanding. His pounding at the door caused me to jump from the pew and my heart to skip a beat. I had nearly forgotten the drawbar locking us inside. I opened it and the wind took it and flung it open, blowing out several of the candles I had lit.

'Shut it!' shouted the Reverend, 'Quickly!'

I did as I was told, throwing the drawbar back in place, and turned to face him. Even in the slender light of the remaining candle flame I could see he was drenched with rain. But it had not dampened his spirit. Quite the opposite.

'Rejoice, Amos!' he cried, his eyes alive with life. 'All the water you can drink! You see how the Lord answers our prayers, brother? You see?'

'Yes, Reverend. Hallelujah.'

'And he has answered yours as well, has he not?' His eyes went to the corner where Rose stood, arms crossed over her breast.

'Yes, Reverend,' I could not help but smile. 'He certainly has.'

'Have you written your vows?'

'Yes.'

'Good, good. Simon won't be coming back tonight, of that I'm sure. But no matter. Paul and Ruth can bear witness. I'll fetch my bible from the house. Paul is putting away Simon's blacksmithing tools; he's left nearly everything where it will get wet. Give him a minute. Relight the candles. I'll return shortly.'

We opened the door again and the wind accosted us, slamming the door open on its hinges and blowing Reverend Mattick's hat off and back into the church. I snatched it from the floor and pushed it into his hands. He put it on and left, running bent over into the blowing gale with his hands clutching it tight to his head.

16

Clouds descended. Dark and thick, hanging low in the sky, they blotted out the setting sun and brought the blackness of night early to the desert wasteland.

Hammond could not outrun the rain. It caught him halfway through the bowl; torrents of water so thick they might have been ocean waves brought in on the backs of angry winds. They lashed horse and rider as if in castigation of some unknown crime. Cannon fire of thunder accompanied the lightning, chasing them over the rusted desert floor. The bolts streaked across the sky in crooked tentacles, some stretching down to hammer what they touched into earthly submission. The jagged rods of light reflected off the clouds above. Their light cast the earth in a silver hue, as if all things physical were made of nothing but stone and lead.

His horse did not falter. It raced in a canter, sides heaving and nostrils flared. They reached the edge of town as one rain-soaked panting emulsification of man and beast. The separation of the two created a wet sucking sound as Hammond swung his leg over the saddle and dropped to the ground. His boots landed in mud.

When the next bolt laced across the sky and the ruins of the Davidsdottir house appeared he let go the reins. The horse hung its head and let the rain pelt its hide.

Hammond walked among the crumbled adobe but no conclusion could be drawn from the rubble. Thunder cracked like a shot from a rifle. His body tensed, expecting an impact. It cracked again and he walked on, past the following house, struggling to listen through the howling wind and the rain drumming down in liquid bullets. Tools lay scattered along the ground and leaned up against the adobe wall. He nearly tripped over them; hoes and shovels and a blacksmith's short mallet, it's handle fallen into the mud.

Turning the corner of the house the church came into view. He waited, watching. Water flowed down the brim of his hat in a steady cascade between his eyes. Rain danced in swirling patterns in the street, lit by bolts overhead.

The church door swung open and Reverend Mattick stepped out. The wind bent his beard over his shoulder and ripped his hat off his head and back into the church. Amos appeared a moment later to shove it back into the hands of its owner. The Reverend pressed it to his head with both hands and ran bent over up the street.

Hammond pivoted around and retraced his steps. He turned the corner of the house and felt the whiff of the end of a blacksmith's mallet as it swung inches in front of his nose. It's iron head crushed the adobe wall on impact.

Les Hammond's hand shot out for a shovel handle leaned against the wall. He flipped it up and swung the curved blade into the man's beard. It struck his chin square, knocking the head backwards and spilling the man into the mud. Hammond rose the shovel overhead and swung down. The metal edge struck the face, carving the forehead away from the eyes. He brought the shovel up again and swung once more. The shovel sunk into bone and remained wedged there, gleaming wet with water and blood.

Hammond drew his gun and continued past the house, around it's corner and into the street. Candlelight seeped through the windows of the Reverend's house. Hammond walked to it, boots squishing into the wet earth beneath him. He reached the door and put a shoulder to it. It fell open and he entered.

Reverend Mattick spun round, a bible in his hands and fear in his eyes.

'Who...' he stammered.

'Where's Rose?' said Hammond. He leveled his gun at the Reverend.

'How did you...'

'What's happened to Rose?'

'Don't shoot me,' the Reverend said, backing away and holding the bible in both hands before his chest.

'Tell me where she is.'

'She is in the church with Amos.'

Les Hammond cocked the hammer back.

'You would not harm a man of God, would you?'

Hammond shot through the bible, knocking the Reverend backwards. He shot into him again as he fell, and once more after he hit the ground. He turned, and had no time but to raise his gun arm against his body as a shield as the prongs of a pitchfork drove themselves into him. One through his shoulder, another cutting into his chest and across a rib, and another grinding along the scapula in his back. The force shoved him against the wall and pinned him there.

The Reverend's wife pushed with all the strength of her thin frame, her aim to shove the tongs of the pitchfork clear through his body and into the wall. Her thin lips curled over her teeth in a grimace, and a thin layer of bubbling saliva glistened on her gums.

Hammond reached his left hand up to the gun hanging in the hand of his pinned arm. He transferred the weapon over and pulled the hammer back, laid the barrel over the backbone of the pitchfork and felt it buck in his palm as he shot into the skeleton body of Ruth Mattick. Her pressure on the pitchfork eased and she staggered backwards. Hammond thumbed back the hammer again. The cylinder spun another round in line with the barrel, and when he pulled the trigger the bullet left the Colt revolver and laid the Reverend's wife out flat and dead on the hardpack dirt floor.

Hammond pulled the pitchfork out of his shoulder. He dropped it and thumbed more rounds into the gun, then left through the door, back into the storm.

He walked down the center of the street. Mud sucked at his boots. Thunder cracked above him in unison with a lightning rod. It lit the street momentarily, throwing light on his saddled horse standing alone and wild looking save for the saddle. He flinched at the unexpected sight of it and continued forward.

Another crack, another streak of white light. The church stood a stone's throw away. The shutters had been drawn closed over the windows. The door was shut. He reached it and looked back to where his horse had stood but it was gone. He held the revolver pointed straight ahead pushed the door with his free arm. It did not move. He pushed harder but the door remained closed. He stared at it, his head swimming, the sound of thunder and wind and rain all about him.

He raised his free arm and turned his hand to a fist and pounded it into the wood.

17

There you have it. I knew you would understand in the end. Remember this, that it is the righteous that persevere.

If only he had come to us with the love of Christ in his heart perhaps things would have ended differently. But he came to us filled with greed, lusting after the wealth of this earth. Thinking of nothing but his five thousand dollars. Did he not understand that man's riches are fleeting? That true fortune lies in the grace of the Lord?

No matter. What's done is done. And for the better I would say. One sinner less in this world.

I am through with Les Hammond. I have no more time for thoughts of him, for my mind is occupied with far greater things. Happier things.

The rain has come. That is good. Our crops will grow and we will not want for water.

But that is only the beginning of our blessings. I wondered if Simon and the women had paused in their work when the rain came. I know I wouldn't. I would keep digging, pulling the gold from the crevice, piles of it, ounces, pounds, a wagon full. I felt my breath rise within me and a rush of exuberance fill my head at the image of golden nuggets, heaped upon the wagon and brought to Santa Fe. Stacks of money, bank vaults filled full with dollars, all of it ours. To do with what we pleased. The things it would buy. The power we would wield.

I wiped my hand across my brow, and brought myself back to the moment. Rose moved in the corner as if trying to distance herself further from me.

Ah yes, Rose. The final blessing. She had not moved from where she stood. Let her sulk. Before the morning sun rose she would know who she served. She was silent now, thank God. She had spoken only once. Her final petitions were nothing more than fantasies of a desperate woman. I had told her to prepare her vows, but she had only scowled at me from the corner.

'Very well,' I told her. I did not lose my calm. 'Sulk all you wish. I will write them for you. And believe me woman, you will fulfill them.'

'I will not marry you,' she said.

'The choice is not yours to make.'

'He will come for me.'

'Who is that?'

'Hammond.'

'Hammond?'

'He will come for me and he will kill you. He'll kill all of you.'

I laughed. 'You foolish child. Les Hammond is dead. I myself took part in his execution. You think we would not find out? Remember this, for it is a lesson you would do well to acknowledge; the righteous always persevere.'

She did not respond. I returned to my vows. They were written, and as I read them I smiled to myself.

Smacks of thunder cracked out in sharp reports. I wished the Reverend would hurry. Such eagerness I doubt I have ever felt before, as I did in my impatience to consummate the marriage.

So long I have waited for this.

I rose and lined the remaining votive candles along the east wall. They took the flame from the match and sent light cascading along the adobe wall. It's red glow upon the clay bricks was truly radiant. Beautiful I dare say. A proper sight for a wedding.

I am truly a blessed man.

The thump of a fist striking the church door cut through the clamor of the wind. Hallelujah, I thought. That must be the Reverend now. I turned from the row of candles and ran to the door and threw the drawbar from the racking.

Made in the USA
Middletown, DE
21 March 2022